Twelfth Moon

Twelfth Moon

Halli Starling

Halli Starling Books

CONTENTS

DEDICATION **vii**
AUTHOR'S NOTE **ix**

1 Twelfth Moon **1**

2 Goats, Drive-Ins, and Boffers **41**

3 Collision **65**

4 Like A Memory Well Kept **83**

5 To You, My Home, I Return **106**

DEDICATION

For those of us who don't see ourselves in fiction. For those of us who need others. For those of us who simply wish to be.

My eternal thanks to my beta readers: James, Leon Tomova, and Precious. You caught every awkward sentence, every missed comma, and your insights were invaluable.

50% of your purchase is donated to The Ozone House (https://ozonehouse.org/) to help with their mission of providing shelter and support to homeless youths and runaways.

AUTHOR'S NOTE

You can read each story individually / out of order! However, many characters or mentions of others cross over and, if you're one of those who enjoys reading in order, you'll get the most out of the varying interactions between characters.

As for the relationships portrayed, they are as follows:

Chapter 1:
Twelfth Moon (Harriet/Dela, f/f; extended appearance by Nu)

Chapter 2:
Goats, Drive-Ins, and Boffers (Nu/Miles, m/m; brief appearances by Jones, Hollis, Audra, and Savanna)

Chapter 3:
Collision (Jones/Hollis, m/m, polyamorous, aromantic, smutty; brief appearance by Evie)

Chapter 4:
**Like A Memory Well Kept
(Maeve /Evie, NB/f; friendship, possibly more)**

Chapter 5:
**To You, My Home, I Return
(Yuri/Beckett, m/f pansexual; Audra/Savanna, NB/f)**

1

Twelfth Moon

"Do we have any more bee balm?"

Harriet poked her head out of the office in the back of the store, peering at Nu's frame silhouetted in the hall. An empty jar was in his hand, one of his many rings tapping against the glass. "There should be more growing in the hothouse." She squinted over the top of her glasses at him. "Trying something different?"

Nu gave an easy shrug, the movement causing his already off-shoulder sweater to droop more. "Curious what a little bergamot might do with the lavender."

"Fill that jar while you're out there and I will pointedly ignore your kitchen witchery." She jabbed a finger at him, unable to stop the smile on her face. "But if I have to clean it up..."

"I know, Auntie." Her nephew's adorable smirk was firmly plastered on his cherubic face and she sighed inwardly. Little brat. Which wasn't at all fair to think about the kid she'd taken in at fifteen and who had only ever been a damn delight.

But she still called him brat to make him laugh, even though he was twenty and in school and working in her shop.

Harriet was loath to return to the land of accounting spreadsheets but her money wouldn't manage itself and it was nice to dust off the business degree every now and then. So when the shop bell rang and granted her a reprieve, Harriet was quick to snatch up her apron and tie it while bustling onto the shop's main floor.

It had been quiet this last week, with the vacationers heading home early when an unseasonable fall frost settled in but she was grateful. Spring and summer were always incredibly busy. They'd often run out of popular items, thus causing arrogant, rich bastards to yell at her and her staff. And since abusing her staff was a one way ticket to getting banned from the store, Harriet had made quite a few fans among the townies of Elsie. The townies kept her business afloat starting in the fall and all through the holidays and winter. After five years, she was a certified townie herself and knew every name, every face.

But the woman with her back to Harriet while she pondered the rainbow hued glass vials in the locked cabinets was a stranger. Not totally odd, given Elsie was gorgeous in the fall and people driving through liked to stop by the diner, maybe meander down the street and wander into her shop or the Coffee Haus next door. The very first thing Harriet noticed was the rich brown of the woman's shoulder-length hair. *Brown* was too plain a word to accurately describe the color and while Harriet inwardly cringed at comparing the color to chocolate, the romantic in her sighed a little. Her hair was lovely, slightly wavy and not weighed down by product.

And she was staring. Right. Shit. Be professional.

"Welcome to The Twelfth Moon!" Harriet said as her footsteps echoed across the scrubbed wood plank floor. She avoided the large knot in one pine board near the main shop counter, like always. She and Knotty had a long standing truce after she'd somehow caught the toe of her boot in it the first time she'd set foot in the space, clattering to her hands and knees while Nu raced over to help her. So Harriet never stepped near Knotty, and she'd not tripped in the store since.

The woman turned, sending her dove gray coat swishing about her knees and Harriet almost gasped. Which was a stupidly dramatic inclination but when those dark green eyes hit her, something zipped down her spine. Harriet blinked rapidly a few times and then smiled like a loon. "First time in?"

The smile she got in return sent another zap down Harriet's spine. "It is," the woman acknowledged. Her voice was clear and even, the kind of voice that could probably carry over a crowd easily. "Your store is gorgeous." The woman waved her hand at the delightfully cluttered shelves and cabinets full of vials, jars, candles, and crystals dotting the rose clapboard walls. "I feel like a witch in an apothecary."

Harriet let a grin slip over her face. She'd heard the line before, of course, but coming from this woman right now, it made her heart flip. "Is there something I can help with or should I pretend to straighten shelves while I watch what you look at and pick up?"

And then charmingly enough, the woman snorted. No elegant laugh here, just unfiltered delight. "My god you're refreshing. I'd heard Harriet Silkman was a straight shooter but it's nice to know the talk around town is correct for once." She crossed to Harriet and put out a gloved hand. "Delilah Atwater. I'm the new head of the nature conservancy."

Harriet took her hand, the buttery leather soft on her rough palms. This day was already going in an unexpected direction. Her shop had a handshake agreement with the conservancy concerning garden use and waste mitigation, so having that yanked away would be disappointing. "I'd heard there was a leadership change. Nice to meet you, Delilah."

Delilah leaned forward with a conspiratorial wink. "Dela's good. Delilah's a mouthful and I have no idea what my dads were thinking."

Harriet's heart kicked up a notch. Another child of queer parents? Her thoughts snapped to her moms' smiling faces; the deep crinkles by Mum's eyes, the laugh lines around Uli's mouth. "It's a pretty name," she said softly, letting Dela's hand go with care. "To be fair, my moms never once shortened my name or gave me a nickname so I like that you took charge of yours."

A pretty flush crossed Dela's full cheeks. "They weren't thrilled at first but eventually my dads accepted that Dela was my preference. They're good like that."

"They sound charming." Harriet mentally shook herself and gestured to the store. "Anything I can tempt you with? We have a few samples out now or I can dab some things onto tester cards."

Dela walked over to a shelf packed with whipped body butters and bottles of lotion, the various gem-hued glasses glinting in the afternoon sun. Harriet never packaged her stuff in the same containers. It had started as a way to save money when The Twelfth Moon was birthed in her farmhouse's kitchen. Buying recycled containers, sterilizing them, and making her own labels had been a learning process but when online reviewers of her shop made all kinds of pleased comments about her environmentally friendly practices and enjoyed seeing what bottles they'd receive, she'd kept up the practice. Always glass, always professionally cleaned, and always lovingly packaged. Everything done by her hand or Nu's or the teenagers from town who were looking for a first job.

Dela picked up a sample bottle and sniffed. Those dark green eyes immediately fluttered shut. "I'd heard your scents were divine but this is incredible." She gave Harriet a keen look, leaving Harriet to stare at the spray of freckles over a sloping nose and across those round cheeks. "Let me see if I can guess....some cardamom, some vanilla." Dela inhaled again, her smile growing in recognition. "Cedarwood?"

"And labdanum," Harriet replied. "You have a very good nose."

Dela snapped her fingers. "Labdanum, of course! It gives it that resiny scent without being piney. This is delightful. It makes me think of being out in a thick forest at night when the last of the campfire has died down and there's still a bit of chai left in the pot over the embers."

Harriet tried not to gape. That was a frighteningly close description of what she'd wanted to create. "Waxing Gibbous," she said, voice suddenly hoarse. "One of the first scents I ever created. Kind of the flagship for the store."

"Well I very much need it but I have no idea in what form." Dela grinned at her and Harriet noticed the little gap between her front teeth. "Any advice for a perfume oil newbie?"

Harriet walked her through the different oils and sprays, since Dela immediately grabbed a bottle of the lotion. She had a standard speech for those new to the way oils worked on the skin and how to understand that they would smell different on each person due to body and skin chemistry. Dela was an attentive student, occasionally lobbing a question to Harriet. Minutes passed and then the door to the workroom shut and snapped Harriet from her reverie. "Got the bee balm, Auntie," Nu said as he jostled the jar at her before noticing Dela. "Oh shit, sorry." His eyes went comically wide and he slapped his free hand over his mouth. "Sorry!" he said, voice muffled.

Dela snorted again, leaving Harriet helpless to withstand how adorable of a noise it was. Rational, logical, stalwart Harriet wanted to slap herself for fawning over a stranger.

In another version of the universe, Harriet the romantic was already asking Dela out for a drink.

Harriet waved him off. "You're fine. Dela, my nephew Nu. Dela's the new head of the nature conservancy."

Now recovered from his faux paus, Nu gave a wave. "Sage is coming up too, Auntie. Nice to meet you, Dela." And then as he was wont to do, Nu disappeared into the workroom to fiddle with the bee balm and whatever else he was concocting.

"Little tip, if you hear any kind of loud bang it's because he's dropped something or has finally made a bomb and we'll need to evacuate." Harriet gave a lopsided grin.

"I like him already," Dela said as she wandered over to another shelf. It took Harriet a moment to realize the woman's arms were full so she thrust a small basket at her, which Dela took with a nod. "All right, I've got my smoky, woodsy scent. Now I need something else…" An elegant hand with a single ring of silver and onyx plucked up a tall, dark grey pillar candle. "Maybe it's cliche but I love lavender. It's so soothing."

Harriet swallowed hard. Dela was unwittingly tumbling down one of her favorite rabbit holes - the science of scent. "It's the terpenes," she managed to say. "Linalool, specifically. I have some info on it if you're really interested."

Dela brightened, her hand already on one of the pre-wrapped lavender candles, the little decorative charm of a leaf on the twine sealing it tapping against her ring. "I would love that! I've always meant to learn more about such things. I have all these plant folklore books at home and get so sucked into the illustrations and pictures that I forget half of what I've read."

Harriet wanted to groan. Could she be any cuter? Her house was packed with books and drying plants and little weird trinkets that probably made the place look cluttered instead of cozy. But maybe it was the kind of place a woman like Dela could appreciate.

Nu bustled in from the workroom with a small tray in

his hands. "Okay, I need feedback and you two are the only other people here." He gave Dela one of his charming smiles and Harriet fought back the epic eye roll that would threaten the elasticity of her brain. "Violet, lavender, bee balm with a touch of honey and the tiniest bit of lemon." Nu set the tray down and poured three small glasses from the already sweating plastic pitcher. The liquid was a deep, velvety purple and Harriet realized she was going to need his recipe for the color alone, no matter whether the tea was drinkable or not.

She waved Dela off as she reached for a glass. "You don't have to, Dela." Harriet shot Nu with a stink-eyed look. "Not all of his experiments are potable."

"Nonsense, it already smells delightful."

They sipped the tea, which was actually delicious, and Nu chattered away with Dela as Harriet neatly wrapped her purchases, taking extra care to make sure all the glass was secure. Her hand hovered over a few sprigs of dried lavender and thyme as she tied the last ribbon.

Fuck it, she thought, quickly tucking the sprigs into the soft silk ribbon. "Here we are."

Dela smiled, eyes going slightly wide at the careful wrappings. "This is lovely, thank you! And you saved me gift wrapping, since that one oil is going to my sister for her birthday."

Then her face dropped. "Oh, shit, I have to get going. What do I owe you?"

Dela paid for her things and once Harriet handed her the lot in a recyclable bag, the other woman smiled once more. This one hit Harriet somewhere near her heart, leaving her mouth dry while something like hope fluttered about in her chest. "It was really nice to meet you both," she said softly. "I'm so new in town that I really haven't met anyone outside of work except Miles at the Coffee Haus. And I'm pretty sure he's nice to everyone."

"He is," Nu agreed dreamily, making Harriet swat at him. "Hey, he is! Hot, too."

The women laughed. "Here." Harriet tucked a few pamphlets on terpenes and a business card into Dela's bag. "If you want more info, I have some book recommendations."

"I would love that." Dela bit her lip and looked down, giving Harriet one final glance at her freckles. "I'll be back, I promise."

And with a wave she was gone, leaving Harriet to stare after her.

"Oh, Auntie," Nu crooned as he leaned forward on the thick wood counter, fingernails rapping. "She's cute. You should totally -"

"Don't you dare."

"What?"

"Don't you feign innocence with me, brat," she teased, making Nu scoff and tousle his overly-long brown curls.

"Are you going to call me brat for the rest of my life?" Nu wrinkled his nose. "I have a name."

"Yes, one I use all the time," she countered. "Especially when you're making a mess of my workroom."

"It was one time!"

Harriet looped her arm in his and pulled him over to the shelves. "Come on, you can help me reorganize these candles for the fall display. And no talking about a certain woman."

"She's pretty, Auntie."

"I see your listening skills have not improved."

Nu laughed.

* * *

That night Harriet sat on her narrow front porch with a tumbler of scotch in hand to watch the mist roll in from the valley. Her farmhouse was technically in the unincorporated area of Elsie Nu jokingly referred to as "No Man's Land" but she liked the quiet isolation. The whole reason for coming to Elsie in the first place was to take ownership of her grandmother's place after her death. While she'd at first chafed at the leaking roof and rotting stairs, the house had been a saving grace. Without it, she would have never been able to take in Nu after his mother kicked him out and she probably would have never started Twelfth Moon. Her tiny apartment in the city had barely enough space for her and her cat, let alone a business and a teenager.

Noodle meowed at her from the window. "Shush, you," Harriet said softly before sipping her drink. The calico batted at the window screen for a moment before settling down to purr. It made a nice backdrop to the croaking bullfrogs and slight breeze that made her pull the blanket around her shoulders closer.

Nu was upstairs in his room writing and occasionally she'd hear a thump as he moved around. But as an hour ticked by and the sky bled from twilight into that vast darkness you could only get out in the middle of nowhere, Harriet sighed.

Her mind drifted back to Dela and her spray of freckles and thick, dark hair. Bright green eyes topped with thick eyebrows, like the ones you'd see in makeup advertisements. Those long, elegant fingers curled around one of *her* candles. Harriet blew out a harsh breath and relented. She'd gone all afternoon and evening without succumbing to looking Dela up online but no one was around to tut at her.

She scrolled through the usual social media platforms but if Dela - Delilah - was on them, she was using a handle of some kind. Just as Harriet got the bright idea to look up the nature conservancy, Nu's footsteps sounded behind her.

"Auntie, what am I going to do with you?" he teased as he shuffled onto the porch to plop down across from her in one of the ratty wicker armchairs. He was draped in a large shawl that covered him from shoulder to knee, the wool soft from years of wear. The shawl had been her grandmother's but Nu had claimed it immediately when he moved in. It made him happy and looked cute on his lean frame, the steel grey with white flowers accentuating his dark blue eyes.

She put her phone down before giving him a blank stare. "Do what with me?"

Nu groaned and slouched deeper in the chair. "Auntie. The woman in the store today! Dela?" His eyes grew comically wide. "I don't usually twist that way but I know you do -"

"I'm not talking to you about my love life, brat."

He carried on like he hadn't heard her outburst. "*And* she was really cute!" Nu jolted forward, bracing his elbows on bony knees. "I've never seen you date. Ever."

The tiny part of her ego that wanted to protest was immediately squashed by the intense concern on her nephew's face. He always wore the saddest little frown when he was worried. "You're right. I don't. I've gone out for drinks a couple of times but it always ended badly." Harriet gestured to her loose sweats. "This is how I spend my evenings. I like being at home, I like the quiet."

"So do other people, Auntie. What if Dela is like that? And if she's not, what if someone else is?"

Harriet shook her head, making a tendril of dark blond hair fall in her face. She blew it away. "I think some part of me resigned to a partnerless life. Long on the shelf, tucked away in the quiet."

Now he scoffed. "Yes, long on the shelf at forty like some spinster in Victorian times." Something flickered over his face, indecipherable and ephemeral at the same time. "Do you think maybe...maybe you're ace? Or aro? Demi?"

She chewed on the inside of her cheek, studying him. "I thought about that," she finally said. "But I experience attraction and I've been in romantic relationships before. There may be something to the demi bit, though." Harriet snorted. "Is there such a thing as a demi lesbian or am I just covering up something else?

Nu gestured to himself. "Twink who can't decide if he's gay or pan."

"Doesn't being a twink mean gay?"

"Says the demi lesbian."

She snorted. "Oh, we're doomed."

Nu arched an eyebrow at her. "Speak for yourself. This twink has a date next week."

"Miles at the coffee shop?"

"Of course." He gave her a shit-eating grin. "And I'll have you know he asked *me* out. I'm done hitting on guys in coffee shops. Flirting with them is fair game, though."

She was going to regret asking this. "What's the difference?"

Nu shrugged. "Approach, language, and the deployment of eyes that scream 'fuck me'."

If she'd been drinking the few drops left of her scotch, she would have spat them right out. Nu started laughing and was soon doubled over. Harriet was helpless when he laughed like that, it was so charming and effervescent and utterly her nephew. "You are terrible. I clearly failed in the teaching of manners," she managed to say, her voice a little strangled.

Nu rose with the grace all twenty year olds have, kissed her on the forehead, then dropped her phone in her lap. "I'll let you get back to your internet stalking."

"I wasn't -"

"You're a horrible liar, Auntie." He winked. "And I love you."

Her heart swelled. "Love you too. Brat."

Once he'd tramped upstairs, Harriet stared at the phone's black screen. It was fair game if it was publicly posted, right?

But she couldn't shake the uncomfortable feeling so she rose with a sigh and took her things inside. Noodle immediately jumped from his spot in the window to curl around her ankles, happy to follow her around as she put away her glass and shut off lights and locked doors. And once upstairs, he took his half of the bed while she fussed in the bathroom.

When she came into the bedroom, with its soft blue paint and bedspread that reminded her of the Mediterranean Ocean, Noodle was on her pillow. "I'm outnumbered by brats," she moaned while the fluffy cat kneaded her pillow.

"Okay, okay, enough. No tiny claw holes in my brand new pillow, punk."

Harriet laid in the dark and let her mind drift over the day, thoughts of the pretty Dela slowly fading to that hazy edge of lucidity one gets before sleep takes them.

Then her phone buzzed.

A notification she should have turned off a long time ago. Confused because of the late hour, she fumbled for the device and then squinted against the sudden brightness.

There was a new comment on an old post from nearly a year ago, when Twelfth Moon was celebrating its fourth anniversary. Harriet stood in front of her shop counter, a basket of what looked like lavender on her arm. The photographer had insisted on using some cheap fake lavender, saying the artificial purple stood out more. She had been poised to hate the photo but it apparently had done enough good to book out her "Science of Scent" classes for months.

The comment read: *Do you still do these classes? I checked the website but didn't see anything. Would be super interested in learning! You've already taught me more with a couple of pamphlets than I've ever known about terpenes.*

The comment was under the profile name of Dela Atwater. Harriet grinned. Maybe Nu was right.

* * *

One week later

"You push that button and there goes your free time for a while, Auntie."

"I know. Hush."

"I'm just saying."

Harriet swiveled in her chair to give Nu one of her patented Auntie looks. "I know you're only looking out for me. But the classes bring a lot of business into the shop and I've got inventory coming out of my ears. So I hope *you're* prepared to work some overtime." She gave him a grin. "Time and a half pay. And grab Yuri, he's so good with wrapping."

Something sly slid over Nu's face. "Time and a half for him, too? He's got a part-time secretary job but you pay better."

She sat back in her chair and steepled her fingers, elbows resting on the chair arms. Yuri was a good kid, best friends with Nu since they were ten and climbing trees and being adorable rascals. His family had moved across town when they were in high school but he and Nu were together almost every day. Harriet liked Yuri; he'd been a good influence on Nu when he was going through a teenage phase of angst, hormones, and hating The Man. She liked to think Yuri's gentle nature calmed her nephew down even in the worst of times.

"Tell Yuri to come by when he's free. I've an offer for him."

Nu bolted forward and kissed her on the forehead. "You're the best."

She waved him off. "You knew that was coming."

"So? It's still important. He's gonna be thrilled." He poked the spot he'd kissed then backed away, grinning. "Who else are you going to give a full-time job to?" And he was gone, bouncing away in battered Converse and black jeans ripped at the knee.

Harriet pushed the button.

Thirty minutes later her first dozen classes over two months, along with their wait lists, were full. Each class took roughly two hours to plan, depending on the difficulty level. First round was an introduction to terpenes and the basics of blending scent, leaving everyone to walk away with sample drams of custom oil blends. The next level up tackled sampling, decanting, and the science behind adding alcohol to an oil blend. And then finally, the master classes sent attendees home with an unrested bottle of perfume spritzer. None of the classes were cheap, but the master level ones were meant for those really invested.

And at two hundred and fifty dollars a head, she could cover supplies for *all* the classes and send some good business to the couple of bed & breakfasts and various restaurants around town. People came from all over for "Science of Scent", which still baffled her.

She was idly scrolling through the list of attendee names when the shop phone rang. "Twelfth Moon, how can I help you?"

"Hey, is this Harriet? It's Dela Atwater."

Harriet's eyes flew open wide as Dela's delightfully smooth voice came over the line. Nu rounded the corner with a box, saw Harriet's expression, and raced over, box nearly forgotten in his excitement.

"Is that her?" he asked, grinning wide and eager.

Harriet waved him away. "Oh Dela, hi!" She bit back a groan. *Sure, sound even more desperate. God.* "What can I do for you?"

"I saw your classes opened back up but was too late to register. Do you know when you'll have another round available?

That way I can be neurotic and put it in my calendar and set an alarm."

Nu was making some kind of strange hand gesture at her and when she stared back, baffled, he huffed. Dove for a pen. Scribbled something on a piece of paper.

"I uh, I'm not sure, to be honest. I usually don't give out much advance notice but you're -"

Nu flipped the paper over. *Give her a special lesson. ALONE.*

And then beside it was drawn a pair of lips.

Be brave, Harriet. Bold. A new Harriet who is still figuring things out but maybe wants to get to know a lady with pretty green eyes.

Harriet cleared her throat before saying, "Tell you what. You were so kind when you came in last week. Why don't we do an individual lesson? But you'll have some homework before AND after."

"Harriet, that's too much. I don't want to skip the line."

Nu was fervently nodding his head. "It's not skipping the line. You had a genuine interest. Not like some of these people who take the class. You know, the ones who pose with a bottle of perfume they made on social media and....I don't know, make duck lips or something."

Dela's sputtered laugh was adorable. It sent a jolt through Harriet's system, that laugh. A little sweet, a little salty. Perfect. "I can't ask that of you."

Harriet smiled, felt it curl on her face and could sense the satisfaction coiling within her. "You didn't ask. I offered. Sound good?"

There was a brief pause. "All right. But charge me extra for the time?"

"We'll see. When are you available?"

Nu was practically vibrating with excitement as Harriet wrote down a date in three days, after the shop closed. Harriet wanted to swat at him for the antics. But seeing the date written down, enshrined on a scrap of paper like some precious thing, made butterflies flutter in her stomach.

When they hung up, Nu raised his arms in victory. "You! You made a date!" He launched into her, squeezing Harriet into a hug that had no right to be as strong as it was.

She huffed into his hair. "This is your fault."

"Uh huh. Sure. Whatever you say, Auntie."

Harriet pulled back to look at him. "It's not a date. It's business."

"It's a business-date hybrid. It can be both. But it's only a date if there's food involved."

The canny look in his eyes made her laugh and hug him again. She remembered that fifteen year old who showed up on her front porch in the middle of a warm fall afternoon, battered suitcase in hand and hair in his eyes. She hadn't seen her nephew in several months by that point and the bruise on his cheek immediately made her vision go red. Her sister's life was always mired in shitty boyfriends and unstable jobs, but she'd always loved Newton.

Until he came out and Gabby's newest shitty boyfriend had a problem with that.

It had never been a question of whether or not Harriet would take him in. And it was all the more telling when her sister didn't try to track Newton down. One tearful phone call and the kid was with her.

Now to see him at twenty, older, wiser, and so full of life, made her proud. He wasn't hers and yet. "Suggestions?" she asked, knowing she had a look on her face that conveyed her mind was elsewhere. Nu called it her waterfall face; every emotion waterfalled from her eyes. He used to tell her that gray eyes were perfect for hiding tears.

"You let me handle that," Nu replied slyly, a wink briefly setting his dark lashes against his cheek. "I gotta run. Yuri'll be in like ten minutes early, knowing him." And he was gone with a kiss dashed across her cheek and a swing of his bag over his head.

Alone in the shop in that dead time between lunch and dinner, Harriet began planning her one-on-one lesson with Dela. Lesson. Not a date.

Even though it would have food.

Shit, she should ask about allergies. Without much thought behind it, Harriet redialed the last number. "Hello?"

Shit. Fuck. But what was she expecting? "Dela? Hey, Harriet over at Twelfth Moon. Sorry to call back so quickly." Harriet could feel her tongue thick in her mouth so she swallowed hard. "I just realized that we set up for around dinner time and thought maybe I could have some food brought in?"

You're rambling, Harriet. Stop. Stop talking.

She winced. Her mouth just kept *moving*. Fuck. "I just uh....it's after work for us both and I know I don't focus well when I'm hungry. So if you hunger - would be hungry! Maybe

I can get Pam at the diner to send something over? But allergies! Right! Allergies, sorry. Don't want to make you sick."

Harriet wanted to groan, put her forehead on the counter, and sink into the floor. Well, that was embarrassing. Time to sell the house, leave town and -

"Harriet, you're so sweet. I somehow knew you were the planning type, what with how beautifully organized your store is." Was she imagining things, or was Dela's already smooth voice somehow deeper? A little more smoky? "And no allergies. But you must let me buy the food. You're already doing me such a huge favor, the personal class and all. And you doing that after a full day of running the shop, I'm just extending your work day. You must let me buy dinner."

Say yes, Harriet. Let someone be nice. But don't confuse kindness for interest. She's simply being nice.

"Okay, twist my arm," Harriet replied, smiling.

"Good. It'll be nice to share a meal with a new friend. If that's not too bold."

I'd let you be bolder. "Not at all. So yeah. Perfect."

"I'll see you then."

"Bye."

Harriet put the phone down just as the shop bell rang and one of her regulars, Mr. Douglas, came in. "Harriet! That time of year again."

She smiled, big and genuine and completely unsure how much was because of his charmingly wrinkled face and how much was due to Dela.

* * *

Three days later - the night of the solo lesson

Harriet was just flipping the switch on the OPEN sign when she saw Dela through the store's big plate glass window. Nu was cashing out a family while Yuri washed down the counters near the tester sink. The family was chattering away with Nu so she chanced a look back. Both boys were grinning like fiends and laughed when they saw her looking. She glared, which made them both laugh harder.

"Insolent brats," she muttered under her breath before pushing open the door. "Dela! Perfect timing."

Harriet reminded herself to not stare at the way Dela's dark jeans hugged her frame or at the glint of a silver chain that disappeared below the open neck of the woman's blue and green flannel shirt. She knew she looked a mess from running around all day but in the hustle of autumn foliage browsers and early holiday shoppers, she hadn't the time to do anything special.

Because it wasn't a date. It was business.

Dela waved and stepped inside the warm shop, brushing past Harriet. The fall wind tried to tease the door from her grasp, giving her a good excuse to turn away and let the cold glass bite into her fingertips. Leaving Nu and Yuri to hustle the family out the door, Harriet focused her attention on Dela, motioning her forward toward the shop's classroom. The shop had been one big space when Harriet bought it but had a section directly in front of the double bank of windows partially walled off. She added in shelves and worktables, more knick knacks and displays, and then painted it a light blue to match the shop's logo.

"I love this." Dela was standing in the open doorway of the classroom and gazing around in wonder, her mouth a soft, pink line that Harriet was absolutely not paying any attention to. She wandered over to one of the built-in shelves, her onyx and silver ring glinting as her hand hovered over the many stoppered glass bottles. Like most things in the store, the bottles were second hand; bought at estate and yard sales, salvaged from the recycling center by Seki, who ran the place and always called Harriet when he found something good. "Gorgeous."

Harriet wasn't sure if she was supposed to hear Dela's

murmur but it warmed her all the same, that hushed word tinged with reverence. "We try to be eco-friendly, as much as possible." She gestured to the garden outside the window. Most of the brightest colors were gone save the gold and burgundy mums, but the winter kale was coming in and the hothouse was packed with sage, rosemary, mint, and lavender. "We grow what we can, resource everything else from ethical sellers. From the source whenever possible, so the money goes to the growers and not some seed company."

Dela smiled. "Preaching to the choir. We try to do the same at the conservancy. Oh, and…." She reached into her jacket pocket. "For you and your nephew. For being so kind to me, and for all the unacknowledged work I know you've done for the org."

Even upside down, Harriet could read "Year Pass" on the laminated slips of paper. The conservancy was a nonprofit, one nearly run into the ground by previous directors, so there was a twinge of guilt in her gut when considering the gift. But the look on Dela's face screamed open expectation.

Dela's predecessor had been a buffoon of a man too worried about making friends at the Chamber of Commerce to run the conservancy properly. Oh it *functioned* but it wasn't the thriving center of education it once had been. Harriet and Nu had done a lot of volunteering there over the years, but for some strange reason the previous director had seen them at best a drain on resources, and at worst competition. A strange set of circumstances for a nonprofit to be mired in, especially when trying to pit itself against a small business.

From the chatter around town and in her shop, Dela was looked upon as a great new hope: young, energetic, educated, passionate. There was something about her and the keen look in those deep green eyes. Harriet couldn't put her finger on it but it warmed her all the same.

Once Dela got settled with wine and food and was seated across from her at the biggest work table, Harriet gestured to the materials laid out. "I thought we'd do a little sniff test first, see what strikes you. Every scent has its own impact on a person. It's like....like finding the perfect moment in a bottle." She flushed. Gods, she was already being too intense. "It's hard to explain."

Dela studied her for a long moment before, slowly, a smile spread over her face. It gave Harriet a chance to admire the way her spray of freckles crinkled. "I was always a tactile person, especially as a child. Touching things, picking them up, sniffing them," she said softly, toying with a vial. The label read "Hallowed Eve" and suddenly, impulsively, Harriet wanted to uncork it and hold it up for Dela to sample.

Hallowed Eve was crisp and heady: dead leaves tumbling over the ground, the kiss of frost on browning grass, and spiced apples and plum tarts cooling on a countertop. She'd made that scent in her grandmother's kitchen and then, hit with a wave of melancholy, she'd broke down sobbing. Remembering the way Grandma's apple pie tasted, how she always burned her tongue in her eagerness to have that cinnamon-sweet taste in her mouth once more.

"And scent is special. So you talking about moments in bottles...." Dela shivered and when she looked up at Harriet, something sparked in those dark green depths. It made her heart clench in anticipation. "I've just never heard someone talk like that before. Out loud. It's like you took that thought right from my brain." She bit her lip, turned away. "I'm not explaining this right."

"You are." Harriet's words rushed from her in a blaze of empathy and something *more*. "You really are. I get it. Truly." She pushed a rack of vials away and leaned forward. "If you could wear the same scent every day, what would it smell like? And I don't mean the notes, like grass or pine. If it's a bottled memory, what does it smell like? What do you want to wrap yourself in?" She saw hesitance flicker over Dela's face and shook her head. "Don't think, just talk. And trust me? I'm actually pretty good at this."

"Okay." Dela was watching her carefully now, her gaze soft, almost dreamy. "I love the woods. Especially when it's cold. Something about the way the air hits you in the lungs.... So a long, early morning hike. Just you and forest. The trees glittering with ice. Snow crunching under your boots. How good coffee tastes in a thermos. And then you go home to a fire and some bourbon and soup. A frayed blanket, a book you keep meaning to read." Dela swallowed hard, her gaze dropping. Harriet mourned the loss of those green eyes on her but it gave her the chance to start plucking up individual scent notes.

Cold air and frost. Firewood and smoke. Dark liquor. The harsh, bright sunrise in the middle of winter, casting diamond sparkle across untouched acres of snow. Old paper.

Harriet plucked up individual notes and brought a handful of rainbow-hued vials over. Their labels were handwritten and worn, but the glass still shone. "Leather and smoked vanilla on a base of teakwood or birch. Old wood scents are heady so we'd go easy there. And on top, fur, ink, and cold air accord." She mixed the vials in the right order as she talked, her smile growing. "Individually they might not smell great, and this might not even be the right combination. The leather might be too strong and we'll need suede, or even cashmere. But we'll get it, I promise."

When Harriet looked up, Dela was staring wide-eyed at her. "You're incredible," she breathed and Harriet felt her face get hot. "I mean that. It's like....magic, what you're doing. Alchemy, even."

"You haven't even smelled the end result yet," Harriet replied weakly. "It could be awful."

"Impossible. I refuse to believe it's anything but sheer magic." Dela pushed up her sleeve and thrust her wrist at Harriet. There was a delicate tattoo of a magnolia on the thin skin, but she only got a glance before Dela was saying, "I put Waxing Gibbous on this morning. That's twelve hours and see? I can still smell it."

So could Harriet. All scents faded over time and would smell different on different people. But after a full day on Dela's wrist, that distinct scent was Waxing Gibbous - vanilla, cashmere, cedarwood. A delicate dessert served near a smoky fireplace but turned soft. Sensual.

Harriet had the insane urge to rub Dela's wrist against her cheek. To put her lips to the delicate tattoo. "It's nice," she finally said, backing away before her strangled voice said too much.

Dela laughed. "So modest. I kept sniffing myself today. I must have looked like a crazy person but it's such a comforting scent." She gestured to the vials Harriet had laid out. "And this will be....I don't know. Me?"

"That's the goal. To find something that's your signature. Your personal scent." Harriet began fussing with the vials, putting them in order of how she'd craft the perfume oil.

Dela's smile softened. "You really are something."

Did her voice have a lilt to it? Something sparking with interest. Flirty even? It couldn't be. Quietly unrequited was something Harriet got used to in her younger years and she found herself flat footed by that feeling once more. It was odd and strange and not entirely unwelcome. But she was indecisive for too long, and with that, the moment passed.

In another version of her life, Harriet took the initiative and pulled Dela to her. Kissed her plush lips. Pushed her against the wall, hitched her jean-clad thigh to her hip, and pinned her there. Made Dela gasp and groan and want more.

A complete stranger was making Harriet lose her head, and she didn't know what to do with all the emotions - and the *want* - roiling through her. So she focused on the lesson, talking Dela through the process. Showing her how to decant the oils, blend them. Discussed letting them rest and how crafting scents was a lesson in patience. Patience Harriet very much needed even as the evening wore on and some part of her desired fiercely.

* * *

The bottle of wine was empty and Harriet's brain buzzed. She was overly warm but her stupid arm was caught in her sweater and she couldn't wrest it free. Damn thing. Damn wine. Damn heat.

She bit back a curse as she twisted her arm and her elbow popped out below the sweater's hem. "Here, let me."

And then Dela was there, with her soft hands. Smelling like wine and wood smoke. Harriet wanted to sink into her, and it was only a little bit of the wine talking and making her think and feel *so fucking much*. But Dela's hands on her were nothing short of a miracle and she sighed as the sweater was pulled over her head and set aside. Cool air rushed over her bare arms but it felt so good to only be in a tank top and jeans. "Thanks. I think it was trying to eat me."

Dela laughed and those eyes flashed at her. When did she get so close? Something swooped low in her belly and Harriet only just avoided colliding with the woman who made her break out in goosebumps. "Shame. The grey is good on you." Dela's round, freckled face softened, her smile even but enticing.

Harriet drank too much wine. That was the problem. Not her ridiculous attraction. The wine was to blame.

"Got hot," she said weakly, grin flickering. "The shop's cold a lot of the time but -"

A gentle finger ran over her shoulder. Over the skin bared by her tank top. "You're flushed," Dela said softly as she leaned in. "Wine will do that."

"Mmmhmm." *Eloquent, Harriet. Good lord. Change the subject.* "I hope you had fun tonight."

"It's like magic, remember?" Dela winked. "How could I not enjoy a little magic? I don't think life is nearly as fun without it." She leaned in. So close. Harriet could feel Dela's breath stir her hair. "And magic's better when it's shared."

Harriet absolutely did not whimper. She didn't lean in as well, eyes firmly locked on Dela's plush lips. She wanted; burned with it. Yearning took on a whole new meaning when the target of your affections was so near, so warm. Looking like she needed to be kissed.

Be bold. Be brave. If she rejects you, then it's okay.

"You're so pretty," Harriet finally murmured. Her hands were cold from nerves but she wanted to *touch*. "I want to kiss you. Is that okay?"

Dela sucked in a breath, her eyes wide. "Yes."

The barest press of Harriet's hand on Dela's arm brought the other woman to her. The ends of that dark, thick hair yielded to her fingers and Dela drew closer. Magnets attracting each other.

Maybe she whimpered but it was lost in Dela's throaty gasp as their lips met. Harriet remembered this - the rush, the adrenaline, the warmth of a mouth pressed to hers. She remembered how good it felt to kiss and be kissed. She remembered she was a creature of flesh and bone, of desire and instinct. Of passion and thoughtfulness. Dela was soft under her hands, delicate under her mouth, and what Harriet had long buried under obligation and selfless love to another came back, bright and burning.

She had once been a creature of need. Capable of loving and being loved. Dela's touch, her kiss, brought that all back. Harriet teased their kiss with the barest touch of her tongue but Dela melted, almost sagging into Harriet's arms.

Maybe they were alike in this way, too. Binding up their need and their passion and locking it away, knowing it would distract from what they had to do day by day.

"Harriet," Dela groaned between kisses, steering them back and back again until Harriet bumped into a table. "Please."

Her knees threatened to buckle. But she had to be certain. Harriet pulled away only to stare at Dela's red lips, the hazy, drugged look in her eyes, the flush high on her cheeks. "What are you asking for?"

Somehow Dela still had the brain cells to laugh lightly and reply. "Anything you'll give me. Gods, I wanted you from the moment I saw you. Stupid, I know."

Harriet stepped into her space, hands going to the other

woman's waist. "Not stupid. There's a reason instant attraction is a cliché. A good one."

A pink tongue darted out and Harriet got caught in the shine left behind on Dela's lips. "Can I ask for more than just sex?"

Something like *hope* threatened to lodge in her throat. "Like?"

Dela was gentle with her touch, her fingers skimming Harriet's jaw. Her shoulder. It made her shiver. Made her crave more. "A date? Dinner, drinks, a walk on the beach?"

She had to grin at that. "You want to sleep together before we do the whole 'get to know each other' routine?"

Dela's gorgeous, round face dropped into a softer expression. The only word Harriet could think of for it was *recognition*. Kindred souls, maybe? Finding their way to each other? It was a romantic fool's hope, but it was hope all the same. "I forgot how nice it is to be touched. Kissed. And from the look on your face a moment ago..." Dela pressed into her, fingers light as air over her skin. Tracing her jaw, ghosting over the thin skin of her wrist. Hovering over her thundering pulse. "I think you felt something like that, too."

"My house isn't far," Harriet replied, voice husky. "My nephew's out on a date, won't be home until late. If at all."

"Yes." Dela's nod was firm, decisive. "Please."

* * *

"I love it." Dela turned in a slow circle, fingers outstretched as if she could touch the air. "Every single thing about this house is perfect."

Harriet chuckled. "You've only been in the kitchen and living room."

Dela walked over to her, grabbed her face, and kissed her. "And I'm sure the rest is just as perfect." Harriet was leaning against a refinished bookcase that had been a summer project years ago, the old varnish stripped and sanded away and the wood now painted a relaxing light purple. "Like this! This is gorgeous." Harriet turned to see Dela pointing at a small lithograph propped on an easel on one of the bookcase shelves. "Is that this house?"

"Yeah, actually. The house was built by my great grandfather and it's been in the family ever since. When Grandma took over the place, she had a friend do that."

"Wow. I just....this place is amazing." Dela leaned in, braced herself on the bookcase. Which meant Harriet was pinned in place. "Pretty sure the presence of the owner makes it even better. My favorite thing in this house."

Harriet blinked. It had been forever since anyone flirted with her, let alone kissed her. She'd heard Dela's desires spoken aloud at the shop, but doubt still wriggled in the back of her mind. "You barely know me," she said, trying to shove the doubt back down. "Are you sure about this?"

"Are you?" Dela's touch to the side of her face was achingly gentle. "I would never want to make you uncomfortable."

The words fell out before Harriet could overthink them. "No, it's not that. It's just been a really long time and I used to think that part of me was gone."

Dela's expression softened, her green eyes going molten at the center. "What changed your thoughts on that?"

Harriet brushed that thick, dark hair back from Dela's face. "Age. Wisdom. Loneliness." Her heart was hammering in her chest at this point. "You. My nephew scolding me for not asking you out immediately." She got a chuckle for that, which made her smile in return. "I'm apparently my own worst enemy."

"A lot of us are."

In that space of a few breaths, Harriet made a decision. She had when Dela first asked but having a beautiful, intelligent woman in her home, leaning into her like this? Harriet didn't want to say. She *desired*, and it felt good.

Maybe she wasn't completely over this part of her life yet.

With gentle fingers, she turned Dela by the chin back to her. "Kiss me."

* * *

Dela didn't leave her house until much later the next day. They spent the morning on the porch, coffee in hand, wrapped in one of Harriet's massive blankets and talking. Every now and then Dela would lean her head on Harriet's shoulder and sigh adorably and every time she did, Harriet got an image in her mind of this being part of their future. Cozy mornings before work, with the rich scent of coffee curling around them. Quiet evenings making dinners together. Long hikes in the forest, snow under their boots and Dela smelling like them and home.

"I don't want to leave," Dela said against her lips as they stood by her car.

"I don't want you to," Harriet replied.

Dela pulled back slowly, those green eyes sparkling in bright autumn sunshine. "Come to dinner with me. Whatever you want. Just....I need to see you again."

Harriet said yes. Again and again and again.

2

Goats, Drive-Ins, and Boffers

"Where are we?"

Miles grinned at him, the expression charming and a little crooked and it made Nu's heart leap in his chest. "You said a picnic was necessary for our first date. So, it's a picnic!"

Nu blinked. "With goats."

"Yep!"

His date was a magician. Or a devil in disguise. Maybe both. He had mentioned wanting to get goats *one time* while talking to Miles over his brother's coffee shop counter, and the blasted adorable man remembered. "It's a friend's farm," Miles explained as he gestured to the open field where dozens of goats roamed behind a sturdy fence. "Her mom and ours were best friends growing up and she moved close to Elsie a few years back. I come out here every weekend and feed the little blighters, play with them. So when I asked, she said yes with no hesitation." A strong hand squeezed his. "Let me go get the food!"

Miles took off at a hurried gait, long legs speed walking him to the big farmhouse in the distance while Nu stared. He was dating a magician. Had to be. Because if Nu thought about it too hard in the moment, he might choke up a little. He'd known from their first meeting a year ago that Miles was special, but it was always one of those things where they talked and flirted over whatever latte Nu was feeling like that day. But it was never more than talk.

He'd been considering asking Miles out on a date (and then got very nervous thinking about doing that very thing), but Auntie Harriet's shop got popular and she needed him more than ever. So between classes and work and not enough days off, he lost track of time and the calendar and all thoughts of asking Miles out drifted away. But Auntie got a crush and Nu realized he'd been so stupid.

So he asked Miles on a date, and here they were.

Nu grumbled to himself one more time, then dumped those thoughts out to make room for the bubble of joy that grew as Miles ambled toward him, a cute rattan picnic basket over his arm. "C'mon!"

He really had thought this whole thing out. There was the checked red-and-white blanket under a tree bursting with fall color; the little containers full of olives and figs, cheeses and crackers. A thermos of water and a flask of whiskey.

And even.... Nu's breath caught as Miles handed him a thicker, folded up blanket. "Wait. Seriously?"

"Well, yeah." But Miles looked away. "I know you said sometimes it's hard to sit for too long and I didn't want you to suffer. And of course if you get to hurting, or are, we can move somewhere else."

"Miles." Nu wanted to cry. No one except his friends and his Auntie understood that sometimes he simply *hurt*, beyond any sense or comprehension. He'd felt like a stranger in his own body for years until Auntie Harriet got him to a specialist and he was told, in no uncertain terms, that he'd probably always have pain but it could be mitigated. Miles knew his body ached sometimes, had probably overheard him talking to Auntie, but the fact that he thought so far ahead and was being so kind nearly made Nu propose marriage on the spot.

Okay, that was a little extreme, but Miles's care was so goddamn sweet and it made his heart soar.

"Is this okay?" Miles squeezed the blanket before Nu took it from him to put under him as a bolster. "I brought the nicest one I could find. I didn't want you to hurt but if you are -"

Nu kissed him. Stupid decision, maybe, to make their first kiss in such a fit of emotion but it felt *right*. Miles had soft lips and smelled like coffee beans and sugar and Nu was struck with another urge; this one far more heated than a chaste kiss on the mouth.

He went to draw back but then Miles was cupping his face, pulling him closer, slanting his lips over Nu's in a way that now really stole his breath. There was a warm flicker of tongue but not too much. Enough to tease, to send tendrils of want curling through him.

"Promise me I can do that again later," Miles whispered as they broke away, panting. "I....damn."

"Yeah. And yeah." Nu laughed and Miles joined in, giving Nu's hand a squeeze before he reached into the basket once more.

"Here," Miles said, leaning in to put a carnation behind Nu's ear. "I thought the red would look good with your hair."

Nu blushed but ruffled his overgrown brown curls, double checking to make sure the carnation was secure. "You have very good taste."

Miles winked at him before pulling Nu to sit next to him. "I got you out on a date, didn't I?"

"Is that more a compliment to me or you?"

And that charming man leaned in to whisper, "Why can't it be both?"

Nu wanted to kiss him. Sitting there in the weak autumn sun, goats romping nearby, and Miles Benewicz in his horn rimmed glasses that accentuated deep hazel eyes in a wide-cheekboned face. And how could Nu forget the adorably crooked nose ("Brother broke it when we were little, told me a whiffle bat wouldn't hurt and I believed him"), the gap in his teeth, or the way he laughed so loud and unobstructed that Nu couldn't help but laugh with him? Everything about Miles was so easy, so relaxed. Leaning back on his hands, grin wide, soft gray t-shirt and jeans hugging his lithe frame.

"These are cool," Nu said, determined to not get too distracted yet. So he waved his hand at the blue studs in Miles's ears. "Are they new?"

"Oh yeah! So you know I help Ms. Meyers next door sometimes, when she needs something heavy moved? She just got these at an estate sale and hadn't put them into inventory yet, so she let me have 'em for the family discount." He grinned and reached for a piece of cheese. "I've been wearing the same ones for ages. Turns out they're labradorite and like, eighty years old."

"I should go in there again to find something for Auntie's birthday."

Nu batted his eyelashes and Miles laughed. "Well apparently I get the family discount so just mention me to Ms. Meyers. Is there anything Harriet wants or needs?"

"I can snoop around and find out. She'd normally say just a card or maybe some flowers but do you think for a second she's a card and flowers type of woman?" Nu scrunched up his face in thought.

"I can't wait to see what you pick out," Miles said, grinning.

* * *

"So that one's Daisy, and this little troublemaker is Spot." Miles brushed his hand over the head of a black-and-white spotted kid who was headbutting his leg. "Ow, ow! Okay, Spot, geez. The one trying to chew on you is Swish."

Nu laughed but was also trying to tug his scarf away from the tiny but insistent teeth of the baby goat. "Why Swish?"

"Oh, Annabelle, my niece, named that one. Said she liked the sound."

"Best reason for a name ever." He leaned back on his hands

and stared up at the cool gray sky overhead. "I love it out here. Thank you for bringing me."

"You bet."

The goats frolicked around them, bleating and headbutting to their hearts' content. Watching them play was soothing on Nu's jangling nerves, and with the reason for those nerves sitting so close, he was torn. It was really a perfect date; relaxed, easy, fun. But Miles was....

Gorgeous, tall, smart, and way too good for me.

"Hey." A warm hand landed on his shoulder, the touch grounding but not pressing or demanding. "You okay? Did you want to go?"

Nu shook his head. "No, I really don't. I just uh...." Gods, everything about Miles was a study in contrasts but at the center, a real heart of gold with a smile that made Nu want to roll on top of him and bite his neck. "You are really amazing."

"Oh!" Miles's smile grew bashful but Nu thought he detected a wicked edge to it. The barest promise of something *else* that had his heart racing. "God, Nu." He leaned in.

So did Nu.

And then a goat jumped in Nu's lap and bleated loudly.

They both burst out laughing while Swish looked completely pleased with herself. "You're a beast," Miles said between chuckles, rubbing the goat's soft head. "You have an admirer, I think."

Nu looked up at him. "Just one?"

"Tease." Miles brushed a soft kiss over his mouth and Nu must have made a noise, because then there were fingers in his collar to tug him closer. "Sure you don't want to get out of here?"

"Oh, fuck." He swallowed hard and pulled back. "Yeah. I think I need to now."

The smirk Miles gave him sent a bolt of heat zipping through Nu's entire body. "Then let's go."

* * *

When Nu stumbled into the pitch dark house, Miles clinging to him and kissing the side of his neck, he laughed softly. "You're trouble."

"I am." And then Miles pressed him into the wall by the front door and kissed him hard. "Thought you liked trouble."

Nu wasn't going to whimper at the growl in his date's voice but it was a near thing. "Hold on, can't see shit -" His thumb found the nubby end of the light switch he was pretty sure went to the lamp in the corner, so he flicked it up. "Ah!"

They both froze as the figures entwined on the couch stirred. His Auntie was dead asleep, dark blonde hair snarled around several throw pillows, one of her many knitted blankets over her lap. And Dela, the woman from the nature conservatory and very much his Auntie's date, was curled in close behind, a flannel-clad arm flung over Harriet's waist. Noodle was curled up on the top of the sofa cushions, his little green eyes winking at him and Miles in the semi-dark of the room.

Aside from being rather grateful they were fully dressed, the entire sight was adorable. He was so proud of his Auntie for breaking down even a few of the walls she'd built over years. "I know it's a bit of a mood killer," he whispered in Miles' ear as they looked at the sleeping women, "but can we go to your place?"

"Hell yeah."

Once they were back in Nu's little electric-powered car, Miles snaked his arm around Nu's neck and reeled him in for another kiss. "Isn't that the lady who is running the nature conservancy now?" he asked, baritone voice sending pleasant shockwaves through Nu's nerves.

He chuckled. "Yeah. I mean, I pushed Auntie but I'm pretty sure the rest of it was all her."

"Good for them."

Miles kept his hand on Nu's knee during the ten minute trip and when they finally got upstairs to his bedroom, Nu couldn't hold back any longer. "God, you're pretty," he groaned before surging into a kiss that felt a lot more serious than it ought to have been for a first date.

* * *

"I don't want to know." Miles snapped his mouth shut dramatically, making his brother roll his eyes. "I know you went out with Harriet's nephew. Good?"

Miles nodded. "Yeah. Thanks."

"Sure." And Jones went back to counting in the till at the counter. They had two registers but only one customer facing. The other was in the back, mainly used for catering orders. Of which there were more and more lately, given the proximity of nearby Hartsford and the number of new businesses the city had added. People drove in from all over for Coffee Haus' coffee and baglenut special.

Miles shook his head and started up the first of his many, many tasks to ready the shop for opening. Jones had never been the most loquacious of people, but they were forty-five minutes from opening, the phone was already ringing, and there were ten customers lined up outside. Miles knew just as well as his older brother how busy their morning was about to get.

It wasn't until the first gap in customers three hours later that Miles realized his brother wasn't ordering him about as much. "Am I missing something?" he asked Mary, one of their regulars and a very old friend of their mother.

"He does seem a little off." She sipped her chai and eyed him over her turquoise rimmed glasses. "And then opposite him, you're glowing. Got someone sweet, honey?"

"Heh. Maybe."

Mary patted his arm. "Good for you. Enjoy that."

The bell over the door rang and Miles straightened to see a tall, lean man in dark grey chinos and a sharp herringbone blazer pause before the menu on the side wall. They got their fair share of new faces in every day, like most businesses in Elsie during the touristy months. But this man was not like the other residents of their little town. He was model gorgeous, sharp cheekbones and sculpted jaw just the topper on bright blue eyes.

He and Mary both saw Jones turn from the till and freeze in place. "Hi there," Jones managed to spit out. Mary's mouth dropped and Miles had to stifle a laugh with his hand. Apparently Jones Benewicz wasn't immune to an admittedly gorgeous face.

"Don't laugh!" Mary whispered loudly, swatting at Miles as he ran by to laugh himself stupid in the stockroom. He'd never seen Jones rattled before and yeah, the guy was beautiful but he was no Nu Marsten. Miles's mind went right back to Nu in his loud sweaters and tight jeans, the glint of antique rings on his fingers. Fuck, Nu was everything Miles had ever wanted in a boyfriend and now he had a chance to fall in love. They'd spent nearly a year dancing around each other but he'd gotten to know Nu in a way that felt special. Felt right.

And this morning he'd woken up to Nu curled against him, arm flung over his waist and a leg wound around his.

His phone buzzed and he pulled it out to see a picture from Nu. It was of Nu standing in front of a new display in his Auntie's store, decked in the store's apron, dark red sweater, black jeans, and combat boots. He was grinning and gesturing widely to the three-tiered display that featured new scents for autumn with a sign that read, "Be Enticing for Fall: Scents to Lure and Ensnare Your Next Love". The display was strewn about with hand-felted roses, garlands of dark red beads that glinted like eyes, and gauzy black fabric on which perched dozens of fake spiders.

He grinned. They'd talked about ideas for the autumn display last night, back at his place, curled up together on the ratty sofa Miles never had the heart to get rid of. Nu hadn't been sure if the spider and ensnaring theme was too much. Listening to Nu discuss his vision for the display was truly remarkable; his mind was a fascinating, mystifying maze of random ideas that shouldn't go together but somehow did. And it was topped off by enthusiasm that Miles found insanely attractive.

"I love it, and I think Harriet will, too."

"Well, you're biased and so is she. What if it scares people?"

"They can buy from your online store."

Nu sighed. "All right. I'll draw it up tomorrow for her."

He was so cute in that moment, hair mussed and lips pursed in thought, Miles had to kiss him. Once, twice, three times and by the third Nu was spread out below him, eager lips on Miles's pulse.

Miles shook himself from the memory when he heard Jones call out. "Need you here!"

"Coming!"

The herringbone coat man was walking out the door, coffee in hand, when Miles returned. "Know him?"

"What? No. Grab that next order."

And so the day went, until Miles stumbled home exhausted. His house was a cute Cape Cod with black shutters and a red front door, but it was all the better for the sight of Nu sitting on his stoop, takeout bags beside him. "Hope this is okay," Nu said as Miles climbed out of his car. "Maybe it's needy or whatever but uh....hungry?"

"Starved." And he was. Miles let Nu inside, took the bags from his hand, and then pressed the smaller man to the front door. His right hand came up to cradle Nu's skull from the cold metal. "Can I have this first, though?"

"Anything. Including your apparent thing with pushing me into walls and doors."

Miles kissed him slowly, savoring the shape of Nu's lips and hitched breaths. "Stay with me tonight."

"Okay. Yes."

* * *

"I haven't been to the drive-in in ages!" Nu popped his head out the car window to look around. "I thought it shut down."

"It did a few years back but Jones went to school with the

new owner." Miles waved a hand at the bright neon sign in the distance. "Haven't been in a while, either. Now..." He shot Nu a cheeky grin. "Snacks?"

The giant tray of popcorn, juice, and chocolate nibs was more than Miles figured they could eat, but Nu insisted - and paid - so he couldn't say no. Nu balanced it between his hands, those rings of his sparkling. One of them, with a deep golden-amber cabochon, was particularly eye-catching. "That one's new. I like it."

Nu beamed and Miles felt it get lodged near his chest. "I went to see Ms. Meyers about some vases for Auntie's birthday. Here, can you..." He gave Miles the tray as they approached his car and Nu dug his phone out of his pocket. "See?" Nu showed him a line of vases, some perfect for tiny buds and single flowers, and other befitting giant bouquets. "She had all these just waiting to go on the shop floor, so we got to talking. Did you know she was a zoologist, worked the primate cages at some place in Connecticut? So cool!"

They got out the thick picnic blankets then settled with their snacks while the crowd milled around them. Nu told him about Ms. Meyer's stories of the gorillas and working with them, how it changed her life and introduced her to her husband. Nu talked about the septuagenarian like she was an old friend, the kindly neighbor with whom you traded fresh produce from the garden and shoveled snow for. "Anyways, I saw this ring on the counter and she said it had sat and sat for months with no interest. So she was going to put it in storage for a bit." Nu held up his hand and let the slowly dying sunset glint red and purple off the large tiger's eye. "It's a little big but at least when I smack my hands on the shop counters, it makes a satisfying thunk."

Miles laughed and snatched one of the juice bottles from the tray. "Doesn't it hurt?"

"Nah." Nu paused with a handful of popcorn halfway to his mouth. "Maybe that explains the weird bruises all over my hands. Huh." And then he winked and laughed at his own bad joke and Miles was smitten. Besotted, even.

They were halfway through the popcorn box when the movie began, and Nu wiggled excitedly. "I haven't seen Nosferatu in forever. I should just buy it."

The movie night was a back-to-back-to-back set of vampire "classics": Nosferatu (the original German film, no other could compare); The Lost Boys; and Interview with a Vampire. "So classic monster, 80s comes to claim us all, and homoeroticism on steroids with a truly delectable Antonio Banderas as Arman," Miles had said as they bought a ticket for the event.

"Hmmm, I love when you say *homoeroticism*," Nu had growled playfully. And then Miles tackled him to the bed and all threads of conversation had been lost. The memory made Miles smile into his drink.

He noticed that as the night wore on, Nu moved closer and closer. And by the time Brad Pitt was saying, "Shall we begin like *David Copperfield*? 'I am born....I grew up.' Or shall we begin when I was born to darkness, as I call it," Nu was running his hand over Miles's knee in a manner that was quite distracting.

"Something you want?" Miles asked as he leaned in. He watched Nu shiver when his breath ghosted over the delicate shell of his ear. "Tell me."

"You." Nu was quick tonight, his fingers clever and grasping Miles by the neck, hauling him forward. The kiss was sharp and full of teeth; the unfiltered desire behind it made his head spin. Nu was smaller than him by half a head and at least thirty pounds, but there was a lot of passion bound up in him.

Miles was just fine being the recipient of it.

Nu kissed him like a man in *need* and Miles tried his best to keep up. Those hands of his fluttered everywhere; touching his neck, his chest, tugging playfully at his too-long, windswept hair. "You don't care we're out in public?" he asked against Nu's mouth.

"It's dark and we can't be the only ones making out," Nu whispered before trailing kisses over Miles's jaw. "But we can stop..."

"No, please."

"Okay."

They missed most of the last movie, so wrapped up in each other and utterly lost in every kiss, every touch. Gods, he was falling hard already. Was affection supposed to make you dizzy and breathless? Or was there something stronger, more permanent pulling at him and his heart?

Nu's hands were under his sweater when someone nearby said, "Audra, leave them be."

"Is PDA in now? Did I miss the memo?"

A musical, female laugh, and then, "Audra."

Miles looked up and saw Elsie's mayor, Audra Bates, and Savanna, their wife, staring down at them. Audra was smiling and Savanna was clearly trying not to chuckle. "Shit, sorry!" he stuttered.

"Don't apologize. I'm just trying to keep the scandalization to the vampires on the screen," Audra said kindly, waving a bejeweled hand at them. "But good for you two."

"Not like we didn't see it coming," Savanna teased as she looped her shawl-clad arm through Audra's. "Have fun!"

They heard Audra say, "Have fun? Seriously, hon."

"What? They were having fun, we interrupted them, and now they'll go have more fun. You remember how we were at that age."

His face burning, Miles looked over at Nu. His date was doubled over, hand cupped tightly around his mouth, shoulders shaking with laughter. "It's not that funny," he grumbled. "The mayor! Oh man, if Jones hears this..."

Nu nudged him with a bony elbow. "You're an adult, and so am I." Even in the low light, Miles could see how his eyes glinted mischievously. "Maybe we should go do adult things at your place?"

* * *

"That is not its name."

"It is!"

"Really?" Nu looked skeptically at the arrow tipped with heavy black foam. "A *boffer*?"

Miles grinned before reaching over to push the dark curls

out of his date's eyes. "I mean you can call it a foam arrow, but boffer just sounds cooler."

Nu snorted. "I don't know about cooler. Weird word." He waved the boffer in Miles's face. "All right, guru, teach me."

"Ah, should we do the whole classic *let me show you how to aim* wrap-around reach?" While Miles was teasing a little, he also moved in behind Nu. Ready to back up if he wanted space or to try on his own first.

But instead he got a hip wiggle and sly grin. "Oh, what a good suggestion. I definitely *hadn't thought of that*. Not me, no way." Nu fluttered his eyelashes and Miles only just stifled his laugh.

"Okay, well, I'm no expert but..." He slid a hand down Nu's jean-clad hip and pointed with his other. "That's the target. You want to hit it."

"Professor Miles Benewicz is in." Nu tipped his head back, ran his fingers over Miles's jaw. "The world's only boffer targeting expert."

Miles snorted but helped guide Nu's arms into place so the bow and boffer pointed toward the target. "Okay, so put your fingers on the end of the arrow like this....good..."

"Do you have any idea what you're doing?"

"Some!" Miles protested between laughs and Nu was reminded, once again, how much he liked Miles's laugh. "Now pull back but use your upper arms and your shoulders, don't bend your wrist." He helped Nu pull the bowstring taut. "Now...let go."

Nu released the bowstring and the boffer flew toward the target. It missed the outside edge by a few inches and skidded into the high grass behind the range. "Whoops."

"No, that was good!" He gave Nu a skeptical look. "Sure you've never done this before?"

It was as good an excuse as any - and he really didn't need one - to haul Miles down by the collar of his thick sweater and plant a kiss on his mouth. "Never once."

"But you had a good teacher?"

"Had?" Nu gave him a faux put-out look. "Going somewhere?"

They shot boffers until Nu's arms tired and he'd hit the target a few times. Then he handed Miles the bow, saying he wanted to watch the expert shoot. Miles brought out the other bow he'd packed, the one that could fire practice arrows that would stick in the target instead of thunking dully against it like the boffers did. He knew Miles was a pretty good shot, but....

The first time Miles pulled back the bowstring, his face dropped into a rather serious, concentrated expression. It made his lovely, full eyebrows draw down but instead of tensing, that cut-glass jaw relaxed, the tension unspooled from his stance. Miles took a deep breath and then...

THUNK

The arrow was sticking out of the target, dead center in the bullseye. Nu gaped at him. "Holy shit."

Something like a cocky expression flitted over Miles' face. "If I'd known a perfectly shot arrow would get your attention, I would have concocted some wild scheme to show off after the first time you walked into the store."

And he'd thought Miles was hot before. "Do it again."

Miles chuckled. "I can't make any promises."

"Do it again anyways."

Miles fired off a dozen arrows before relenting; half of them were sticking out of the middle of the target with the others close by, some edged out of the bullseye only by the lack of space. With every arrow, Nu's mouth dropped open a little more; by the time the quiver was empty, he was pretty sure he was catching flies with his gape, as his Auntie might have said. "Holy shit," he breathed again.

Miles dropped his arms and let the bow dangle from his fingers. "Eh, I've done better."

Nu pointed at the blanket they'd spread out on the grass a safe distance away. "If you don't get over here and kiss me right now, I'm going to need to tackle you."

Miles was warm against him, the worn cuffs of his sweater brushing against Nu's neck as Miles cupped his face and slotted their lips together. "I would have, you know," Miles said softly when they broke apart. When Nu gave him a confused expression, he said, "Found some way to impress you. I'll never get that day we met out of my head. We were so busy in the afternoon but I swore everything kind of...paused when you walked in." He flushed endearingly. "Fuck, that's cheesy."

Nu shook his head, blew his curls out of his face. "What's wrong with cheesy? I *like* cheesy."

"Ouch." But Miles was grinning.

"But since you brought it up...I was wondering why it took us so long to do this." Nu gestured at the field. "We kept flirting but we never did anything about it. I mean, I know why for me but -"

"You scared me." Miles' words were slapped together, as if he couldn't get them out fast enough. "Fuck. Okay, I mean, the thought of maybe having something scared me. We just got along so well so quickly, but we were always out with big groups or bumping into each other around town, and then you were coming in almost every day and I..." He sighed, put his hand on Nu's knee and squeezed. "I've not really done the whole dating thing. Here and there a bit but you feel *right*. I know that sounds insane."

"Miles."

"Yeah."

Nu felt like his heart might burst from his chest at any moment if he didn't spit this out now. "It's not insane. It does feel right. Guess I should just ask, then." He picked up one of the boffers and held it up. "This boffer as my witness, I'm asking you if you want to be my boyfriend."

Miles stared at him for a long, fragile second before pulling Nu into his lap, discarding the boffer to the side, and kissing him. "That's a yes, if you couldn't tell."

"I think I got the message."

"Good."

3

Collision

"I thought you....said...you wouldn't come in the shop."

"Yeah well...I lied."

Jones groaned and let his head thunk back against the wood of the headboard. Hollis had the *perfect* mouth and he had no problems letting him know that through a chorus of moans and panted words. One thick arm was thrown over his hips, pressing him down into the mattress even as he bucked into hot, wet, insistent pressure. The other hand was roaming up his stomach and chest, pinching, flicking, caressing.

Jones was in heaven, or whatever approximation of it involved Hollis's bright blue eyes, sinful mouth, and utterly lickable body. He could barely eke out a moan for the pleasure rattling up and down his spine. The man was a blow job *god*. Jones thrashed under Hollis's talented mouth and hands, his body clenching in that liquid desire kind of way.

"Close," he panted out, eyes squeezing shut as another

shiver of pleasure licked like flames over his skin. That soft, wet heat left him and he groaned his displeasure, but Hollis was there, pressing kisses into his hip while a hand took over. "Ah, fuck."

The laugh from Hollis was a rumble of sound and air against his skin and it made Jones grip the sheets. "Look at you all flushed and sweaty," Hollis purred, blue eyes dancing with pleasure. "So pretty, red like that."

Gods, that shouldn't have turned him on but it did and Jones was *lost*. He groaned through his release, vaguely hearing Hollis whisper, "Good boy," into the sensitive skin of his side.

He came back a few minutes later, still shivering from oversensitivity and the chill in his room. The fire had nearly gone out and Jones hadn't yet turned on the heat, so the heavy autumn rain was seeping into the air. But that's why blankets existed; so he didn't have to get out of bed before seeing to his partner. "What do you want?"

Hollis flopped down beside him with a lazy grin. "I'm good."

"What?" Oh no, he never left a partner unsatisfied. And he knew for a *fact* Hollis squirmed in delightful ways when speared open on three fingers.

"I'm good, I swear." Hollis licked his lips. "Fuck, I can still taste you."

Jones groaned, the sound turning into a laugh as Hollis made exaggerated smacking sounds. "Stop. Gross."

"I'm going, I'm going." With liquid grace, Hollis stood and stretched. Then shot Jones a stare, complete with arched eyebrow. Jones let his gaze travel over his partner's lean back and down over his ass. "Besides, if I don't rinse this you won't let me kiss you."

Jones caught the tissue box he was tossed, giving himself a few swipes before sitting up. He needed a new mattress badly; even sex on the bed left him achy instead of fully satiated. With a roll of his neck, he got to his feet and went into the bathroom, slipping behind Hollis. "You sure?"

Hollis leaned back, content to let Jones press kisses into his neck. "Yeah. Head's been bothering me all day. Just wanted to get you off."

"And you did." Jones placed a final kiss below a sharp jaw-line. "But don't think I forgot the whole coming-into-the-shop deal."

Hollis laughed, the sound rich and almost luxurious. "You told me you didn't work counter in the mornings and I was running late and under-caffeinated. And it was for my boss so..."

Jones laughed with him. He wasn't really angry or upset. He knew Hollis's boss was a hardass who liked his things *his way* and if he'd asked Hollis to go get him coffee two towns over, that's what paid the bills. Hell, shitty bosses were most of the reason he'd finally opened his own place. He'd seen all the mistakes business owners made and vowed to not fuck up like them. And so far, that had worked just fine for the Coffee Haus. It was paying the bills and putting Miles through college and letting him pay for their mom's cancer treatments.

If this had been when Hollis first moved near Elsie, Jones would have balked. They probably would have argued. Not everyone would understand their casual arrangement, and since some of the overbearing retirees near East Village thought Jones was the perfect target for their newly divorced or unmarried adult children, Jones was glad he didn't have to lie when he said he was *with someone*.

He was with several someones, but Hollis was his friend as well, from as far back as university. Most of the others were occasional flings when they were in town or in the mood. He had only a few rules: no serious monogamists (dating, engaged, married and so forth), no ideals that clashed with his own (aka bigoted assholes need not apply), testing and protection required. And he was upfront about having multiple partners. Jones liked sex and he liked having the variety of people he slept with, but Hollis was only one of a few he'd been friends with first before getting physical. Others, like Mason, were in the same soccer league as he. And with Mason it had been hookups in the showers or the backseat of his car after games, but a friendship had developed there. A good one, too.

Jones wasn't made for romance. He figured the more emotionally involved, the messier, and he wasn't about to empty out a drawer or clear space in the bathroom for someone, let alone circumvent his own routines for someone else. Some people called him "selfish" but Jones saw it as practical. Some people wanted a spouse and two point five children; other people wanted to be left the hell alone. Needing physical affection and sex didn't mean he had to get invested, emotionally or spirtually.

"Then I trust that. And you." He gave Hollis's ass a slap as he moved by, earning a wiggle in return. Shower heating up, he watched as Hollis rinsed his mouth, then ran a hand down his throat. Teasing. "Ugh, gods, you're going to kill me," he groaned, sagging against the wall. His dick was *very* interested in the sinewy, handsome man just feet from him.

Hollis shook his head, blonde hair flopping over his forehead with the movement. "Shower, you're sticky."

Jones swatted at him, missed by a mile, and stepped into the shower. "Be better if you got in with me."

Hollis was across the room in three steps, looping an arm around his neck. "And I told you I had two hours free this afternoon before I gotta go back to work."

"Hmmm, did it work?"

"What?"

Jones grinned. "Sucking me off to relieve your stress?"

Hollis barked out a laugh. "Yeah, actually. It did."

"Lucky me. And I owe you."

Hollis gave him a heated smirk. "Yes, you do." He kissed Jones with enough tongue to make his dick twitch, then stepped away. "Be good, you."

They didn't see each other again for a few weeks, Jones running the shop keeping him constantly busy and Hollis's asshole boss sending him across the country for a workshop on less than twenty-four hours notice. They kept up like they always did, over text and social media, sending the occasional message or picture (including Hollis's tendency to text him shirtless pics at two in the morning when the man couldn't sleep).

Hollis wasn't even in town for his own birthday but Jones promised to take him out once he was back. And on a Tuesday night he got a text that said, "I'm finally fucking home. And I want to fuck. Can I come over?"

Jones fought back a groan. He was out with Ticia, one of a few women he maintained relations with. They always liked to go to dinner or out for drinks before stumbling into his townhouse, laughing and pulling at their clothes. Ticia was special; they'd gone to college together and their sex dates had started then. Ticia was the first person to not treat him like a broken weirdo for wanting sex but not romance. Well, a weirdo or a player. And he definitely wasn't insulted by "weirdo" but heavily was by "player".

She also knew him well enough to see the remorse on his face as his finger hovered over his phone's keyboard. "Especially hot piece?"

"Huh?" He jerked his head up to see her grinning at him. "I'm out with you, Tish."

"Uh huh. And I know that look, like someone kicked your dog."

"I don't have a dog."

"The sentiment still stands, J." She wiggled her fingers at him. "Lemme see." He handed her the phone and then she grinned. "Oh you lucky bastard. I didn't know you and Hollis were still..." She made her cheek pop out with her tongue and laughed.

"Have you seen his cock?"

"Sadly, no."

Jones slumped in his seat. "Incredible. Just incredible."

Ticia pouted playfully. "You say that about my tits, too."

He gave her a gently admonishing look. "Your tits are incredible. And you didn't laugh at me when I asked if it was okay to refer to them as 'tits'." Ticia just laughed harder, drawing a few looks from nearby tables but neither of them cared. Jones tended to think that people who stared at those clearly having a good time were simply jealous.

"Are you gonna text him back?" she asked as their waiter brought a fresh round of drinks. "You shouldn't keep a man with a great dick waiting."

He stared at her for a moment then nodded, unable to wipe the growing smile off his face. "Okay, okay! But we're still out, Tish."

Her eyes sparkled. "And you I can see any time I want because I work across the street and I'm in your face at seven a.m. daily for coffee. Buy my drinks and I suppose I can forgive you."

With a fiendish grin, Jones fired back a quick message: *Sorry, out with Ticia but she's given us her blessing.*

"Remind him he's seen my tits," she said over the rim of her martini glass.

Jones snorted but continued his message: *She says to remind you of her great tits, which I'm guessing is her way of saying you're welcome?*

He'd barely set the phone down before it pinged with a response: *Tell that woman I love her and make sure you eat before you come over. I need you in me at least twice.*

He pushed the phone at her and watched her face light up with glee. Definitely not the ending to the night he'd been expecting but he was not going to complain. Ticia left him after another round of drinks and appetizers with the bill, a slap on the ass, and a filthy kiss while she was pressed up against her car. "Go get that D, babe," she purred out the driver's side window before peeling out of the parking lot, the tires on her Mustang squealing.

Fuck, he was already half hard and he had a forty minute drive.

* * *

He wasn't even in the front door before Hollis had him pushed up against the wall, a long-fingered hand under Jones's shirt and the other in his hair. "What's got you riled?" he asked, nearly cross-eyed watching Hollis kiss his chest and trying not to writhe.

Hollis nudged the door shut with an elbow just as the first crack of thunder sounded overhead. "I hated that trip so much. It was pointless and boring and I had to skip our usual booty call."

He laughed and pulled Hollis closer. Something quiet but beat-driven, almost slippery, played on the speakers in the next room and he felt it between his ribs as rain lashed the nearby windows. "Remind me to thank your boss, then. More boring trips means I get more handfuls of this ass." Jones slid his hands down and squeezed. Hollis sagged against him with a groan. "Come on, not gonna fuck you standing up."

They threw clothes off as they went down the hall to Hollis's bedroom, bumping into walls, laughing between kisses. Gods, Hollis felt so good under his hands; warm and firm, his hair growing out long enough that Jones could get his fingers into it and pull. "Should keep it this long. Hell, grow it out, past your shoulders" he growled. Hollis moaned, eyes fluttering shut and he suddenly had an idea. "You like that?"

Hollis gripped his left arm with both hands. "Yes. Fuck."

Another tug exposed Hollis's throat and Jones made himself busy nipping at the sensitive skin there. "Should have said something. We both gotta enjoy this -"

"I do! *Ah fuck*. Don't stop."

"And yet...." He lifted his head and got a good look at his lover's flushed face, the teeth sunk into his lower lip. "If you want something, tell me. I'm open to experimenting." And then he leaned back down to whisper in Hollis's ear. "I'm out of practice but I used to be quite good with rope."

Hollis all but pushed him down the hallway and threw him on bed, eager hands and hot mouth on him a second later. Jones was happy to let Hollis strip them out of their clothes but when he suddenly got up and walked over to the wardrobe, Jones sat up. "Something wrong?"

A bit of silk hit him in the face and he plucked it up between two fingers. He was rather familiar with the belt and the robe it came from. "Not at all." Hollis crawled onto the bed and over Jones, caging him in. "I want you to tie my wrists."

Lust pounded in his veins even as his mouth went dry. Would Hollis just....let him do this? Sure he'd done it before with other lovers, a little vanilla kink on the side to add a bit of excitement. But the man's eyes were shining with interest and

Jones realized there could be an entire wellspring of want hidden behind severe cheekbones and dark blonde hair. "Don't want to jump to ropes yet, huh?" he teased as he let the silk robe belt brush Hollis's arm.

Hollis flushed. "I just want you to....do what you want. With reason, of course."

"With reason, sure." Jones brought his hand up to cup a firm jaw. "You sure about this? When Hollis nodded, the next question was easy. "I need a safeword. I won't do this without one."

"Tacky."

His mouth twitched in amusement. "Done this before, have you?"

Hollis laughed. "Not for a long time. But I trust you. We've been fucking for...what, almost a year? You get me, Jones. You get needing physical affection but not being interested in love. You never get offended that I don't stay over or ask you to stay at mine. We meet for dinner, we fuck each other's brains out, and..." He smirked. "And you answer my booty calls. Your call to fuck ratio is better than anyone else's."

Jones snorted. "Oh I like that. Call to fuck ratio, that's good."

"Thought you might." Hollis rolled off him and flopped onto his back, arms up in invitation. "Now, get to it."

By the time Jones had left a trail of red love bites down Hollis's chest, the other man was squirming and panting and hard as a fucking rock. And other than brushing against his erection on occasion, Jones didn't let him have any friction. He'd ask if it was still okay and Hollis's increasingly breathy answers in the affirmative left him smirking. Some little bit of his ego was pleased to see he could still drive someone crazy with just his mouth and tongue.

Jones planted a kiss on the inside of Hollis's hip, teeth grazing the spot a moment later. Hollis was whimpering, thrashing. "Behave," he warned, keeping his tone warm. "Or you don't get what you want."

"Want you in me," Hollis panted. "I need you to fuck me."

"And I need you to be patient," he purred back, letting Hollis feel the strength of his fingers pressing on the inside of his thigh. You didn't make complicated coffee drinks day in and out without gaining some decent hand strength and dexterity. "I thought you'd want to be teased. All tied up like this and everything."

Hollis actually *whined*, a needy, desperate noise that almost made him give in completely. He arched against Jones, a long, sinuous line of flushed skin and smelling like the remnants of a cedary cologne Jones knew well. He pulled Hollis up by the neck, smashed their mouths together. Without the use of his hands, Hollis was left to Jones's desires. He knew Hollis would say something if things got uncomfortable or awkward; he trusted the man like that after countless nights with one of them pinned to the mattress.

Or floor.

Or on one very memorable occasion, to the daybed in Jones's tiny home office.

Daybeds were not meant for rigorous fucking. The rickety thing had given out almost immediately but that hadn't stopped them.

"How bad?"

Hollis was already looking out of his mind, *wrecked* with need. "What?"

Jones kissed a muscular inner thigh, liking how it quivered under his touch. "How bad do you want me?"

* * *

"You should totally ask him out."

"What? No, Evie, just because I said I think he's hot

doesn't mean I'm going to ask out a complete stranger *at his work.*"

"Yeah, well, you need to live a little. And as your sister, I'm saying do it."

The pair were having a discussion not feet from the shop counter but they were acting like there was no way Jones could hear them. *Everyone* could hear them; it was a small shop. Only the banging of cups and the hiss of the espresso machine disguised any conversation but for hells sake.

The man was probably in his early thirties, with dark, shiny hair pulled back in a bun. His flannel shirt and jeans and boots screamed money, but the rolled up sleeves, forearm tattoos, and ears dotted with silver studs spoke of rebellion. Interesting. The woman he was with was clearly a relation, but he would think that even if he hadn't overheard *sister*. She had the same dark, shampoo commercial hair and pointed, patrician nose, but was a half a head shorter and dressed warmly in a thick red sweater and black jeans with knee high boots.

"Hey," the man said with a grin. Jones noticed the brown eyes, the long lashes. Some people were just genetically gifted. "Uh, can I get a macchiato? Evie?"

"Yeah, hot cider?"

Jones smiled at them, gave them their total, and motioned

to the little waiting area as the man paid. The sister stepped aside, Jones handed the man his card back and then -

"Yeah so uh, can you do me a favor?" The man gave him a tight-lipped smile and lowered his voice, his eyes darting to his sister. "Just say, 'Oh, sorry, I have a boyfriend'."

"But I don't." Jones frowned at him. "Have a boyfriend. I don't date like that."

Something like....recognition lit up the man's face. "Yeah, me either. But try telling her that."

"Have you *tried*?"

The man scoffed. "It's that easy?"

"You told me, and I'm a complete stranger."

"Right. Okay yes, fair point and I'm an idiot." The man stuck out his hand. "I'm Niall."

Jones took his hand with a smile. "Jones."

"I'm his sister, Evie!" the woman yelled from the side, her grin so wide it threatened to split her face.

Niall groaned. "Sorry about her."

Miles came out of the back room with an armful of stacks of cups. "That's mine," Jones said, hooking a thumb at his brother.

Miles tried to shoulder-check him but Jones dodged out of the way, making Niall laugh. "So, Jones....what's there to do in town?"

He never was one to say no to opportunity. A new face, maybe a new friend. Maybe something else. Jones ripped off a piece of blank receipt tape and scribbled an address down. "It's a speakeasy not far from here. Good drinks, live music on the weekends. I know the owner. Tell Maeve you know me when you go."

Niall took the slip of paper as he said, "And if I show up say, tonight, you might be there?"

This wasn't the strangest way to meet a potential partner, but as luck would have it he and Hollis had just discussed adding a person to their arrangement. "I might. Might be with someone. You should join us."

And damn it all if Niall's eyes didn't light up with interest. "Then maybe I'll be there tonight."

"Good." Jones grinned. "Wear your tightest pants."

"Oh, really?" Niall was smirking and it was an adorable

expression on an otherwise severe looking face. He reminded Jones of a bird of prey, like a hawk. "For you or…"

"Both of us. But he's the one you'll have to win over, not me."

The slip of paper disappeared into Niall's back pocket. "I think you'll find me very persuasive."

Jones got them their drinks and with a nod to Evie and a wink at Niall once her back was turned, he watched them go. It was always nice to know you weren't alone.

4

Like A Memory Well Kept

Friday nights were always the busiest, but Maeve was glad for it. It had been a tough month and an even tougher week, but at least after tonight, they had all weekend to relax. Aching muscles screamed for a hot bath and their exhausted mind just wanted stupid movies with about a gallon of ice cream.

Maeve put the beer down in front of Garrett, one of the speakeasy's regulars. "All right?"

He nodded, very serious blue eyes tired behind rimless glasses. "Yeah, yeah. I'll catch you when things slow down."

Maeve laughed. "You mean *if*. It's Friday night happy hour."

Garrett raised his glass to them. "Then cheers."

Maeve hoisted a shot glass high, threw it back, and headed to the table that was just sat. A woman with thick, glossy hair piled high on her head was staring at the drink menu with studious concentration. She looked strangely familiar, but Maeve figured the woman just had one of those faces.

She was also very pretty, but Maeve wasn't going down that road. Especially not tonight.

"Welcome to The Lamplighter," Maeve said as the woman looked up at their approach. "I'm Maeve. Been here before?"

The woman smiled, her eyes going to the "They/Them" button Maeve wore next to her name badge. "Actually, no. I kind of thought this place was a myth. The speakeasy in the basement of an antiques shop. Like I'd need a code word or something to get in."

Maeve snorted. "I honestly thought about it. But making people looking for a drink jump through hoops seemed a bit much." They motioned to the drink menu. "Want a run down of the list? Or, if you want, Carter can make you something based on how you're feeling in the moment."

"Oh, now that sounds appealing." The woman leaned forward, hazel eyes behind thick, black-framed glasses suddenly bright with interest. "Let's do that."

They nodded. "I'll send him over."

"Actually, let me move to the bar. Don't need to make y'all run back and forth."

Maeve watched the woman rise from the little booth with fluid grace and walk over to the long, polished oak bar and take a seat on the far left end. Well, that was...surprisingly civilized. Most of the folks who came into The Lamplighter were polite and their regulars were as close as Maeve got to seeing friends from Friday to Tuesday. But this woman, this stranger, was nice and chatty from the outset.

Maeve shrugged and went back to the bar, tapping Carter in to go talk to the woman so they could focus on filling orders from the already bustling tables.

Time passed like it always did on Friday nights - in a blur that kept Maeve so busy they didn't even notice the hour. Today it was extra needed, that passage of time, to keep them from lingering on old memories. They pulled beer after beer, made martinis and sours and uncorked dozens of bottles of wine. The cash register chimed, trays of clean glasses still warm from the dishwasher were brought up front, and they moved through the motions of the night like any other.

"Hey."

Maeve blinked, looked up. That woman was in front of them, but her pretty hair was undone around her shoulders and her cheeks had a slight pink flush to them. "Hi. Last call's not for another hour, if you wanted something else."

"Oh, no. Sorry. I uh, left a while ago but left my phone here like a dummy." She nodded at Carter, who waved. "He found it for me and put it aside."

Maeve had to laugh. "He's got a knack for finding things people lose before they get stolen. Glad we had it for you."

There was a hesitance on the woman's face now, and she opened her mouth a few times before saying, "I'm kind of new in town. I'm Evie." And she put out her hand.

Polite. It was nice. "Maeve. Nice to meet you."

"I remember. Your name, I mean! And yeah, you too." Evie quirked a grin at them. "Weird question...do you know of any good hiking spots around here? I figure with all the hills and forests, there have to be some good places. Thought I'd ask a friendly local."

Maeve put a hand over their heart. *Friendly local* didn't mean much, but the sentiment was nice enough. "You're hitting me where I live. Elsie's one of the best places in the state for hiking. There are a ton of spots, depending on what you're looking for. The parks have really good trails, so I'd start with their website and then use a trail app to mark the trailheads."

Evie beamed. "Yes, that's perfect! Thanks a ton, Maeve." She slid a twenty over the bar. "Please. The drinks were amazing and you have a really nice place."

Maeve nodded and pocketed the twenty, already mentally marking it for Carter when he came back from the stockroom. "I appreciate it. Things get a little nuts here on Friday nights but I'm glad you enjoyed it."

"I did. And thanks again for the info." Evie gave a cheery wave, then bounded out the door and up the stairs. A moment later she was gone and Maeve was left with another round of dirty glasses to take back to the kitchen.

When they got home around two in the morning, Maeve collapsed on their sofa, kicked off their shoes, and watched the light from the fish tank cast an eerie blue glow over the room. Friday nights were always exhausting, but sleep eluded them. What would be smart would be to go down the hallway, change, and fall into bed. Instead, Maeve pulled a blanket from off the back of the sofa and over them, only remembering too late that it had been the blanket Stella had made them for their first wedding anniversary.

Maeve cried until they couldn't anymore and didn't bother washing their face before falling asleep.

* * *

The ritual of packing their gear, checking the charge on

their phone, and loading trail maps was soothing. Every year, this simple rhythm did something to ground Maeve. It was a rebalance of how increasingly off-kilter they felt without Stella. Years had passed since their wife's death and yet as the anniversary of that day loomed large on the calendar, Maeve felt that wound open once again. They'd long ago accepted that they'd never be the same after losing Stella and even as time moved on, they felt a little stuck. The same routine day in and out, the same life.

Stella died five years ago, two months after Maeve's godfather. Cadmus had raised Maeve and they had never once felt like anything but his child. So losing him and Stella within weeks of each other had been almost too much to bear. But they were here, and another year was gone, and for the first time Maeve wondered if there was something they were missing. It tugged at them in the dark, cold hours of night when they couldn't sleep for the sake of wanting to feel Stella's warmth next to them one more time.

Just one more time. Was that so much to ask?

Maeve sighed and, with a fingertip pressed to the worn silver ring on a chain around their neck, hauled their gear to the car. Knowing the drive by heart didn't mean they could zone out during the trip, but the coffee in a travel cup, the music playlist, the familiar feel of the worn steering wheel made focusing easier. Maeve didn't drive for nearly a year after Stella passed and still kept to the roads they knew well.

But like every year, the drive passed in a blur and what seemed like mere minutes later, they were standing before the Bear Hook trailhead and breathing in the scent of cold pines and decaying leaves.

Their bag was a familiar weight on their back as they climbed the first of many small hills leading up to Bear Hook Point; the highest in the county and one of Maeve's favorite spots on the entire planet. They focused their senses on the ground beneath their feet, the sound of birdsong in the air, and even the steady thump of their heart as they climbed. In the chill of a late autumn morning, they felt connected again. Set back on track. No longer off-kilter and tipping, tilting at a dangerous angle.

Every year they did this because every year she was still gone.

It wasn't even noon when Maeve slipped around the boulder into which Stella had carved their initials. They'd been dumb, giggly high schoolers, too enamored with each other and the blush of first - and eventually only - love. High school sweethearts getting married young was a nice trope, but in reality it rarely worked. People had a lot of growing up to do in their twenties and by statistics alone, they and Stella should have split up around the time Stella's mom died. All that stress - college, exams, death - it should have broken them.

It had made them stronger instead.

And then Cadmus had died and Stella had been there, helping them do the lifting of the funeral and estate nonsense. And when she was taken from them, the entire world fell off its axis. They went to therapy, found a support group, made new friends, kept the bar going. But all perfunctory.

Now perched on that boulder and looking over the vast valley in which Elsie sat, Maeve admired the glitter of the ocean in the distance, the sun-dappled waves a mere suggestion but beautiful anyways. Maeve sighed and let themself sink into good memories of those years with Stella.

* * *

Evie came up the hill at a quick pace, eager to see her new home from such an incredible vantage point. But the figure on the boulder up ahead gave them pause. Something about the cloud of curly, dark hair struck her as familiar. But that could be dozens of people in Elsie alone, with a mass of thick curls that sprang out at all angles. Just yesterday she'd asked a woman with gorgeous hair dyed several shades of an ocean sunset where she'd gotten it done; the woman's hair was thick and curly and she'd proudly given Evie the salon's name.

No, it was something about their posture. Most people perched on the top of a rather large boulder would spread their stance, balance their weight. Instead, they were seated at the very top, on the very edge, booted feet dangling, spine straight. Alert, attentive. And they turned their head and saw her.

"Hey!" Evie waved. "Maeve, right? From the Lamplighter?"

Maeve smiled slightly and held their hand up in greeting. "You have a good memory."

Yes, for attractive people with a certain air about them that makes me want to stand at attention and earn their approval. "Your bar has some of the best drinks I've ever tasted."

"Glad to hear it."

Evie blinked. Waited. Just as Maeve sighed, Evie realized they'd intruded. They hadn't been meditating or taking a photo of the view; they'd been focused. "Sorry," she said quickly as she backed away. "I messed up your moment."

The smile was gone but there was now a little nick between Maeve's brows. Their sunglasses hid their eyes and Evie wished she could read them better. Read people better in general actually, as she was usually shit at that. "It's all right." Maeve turned their head to look back at the valley below. Evie could see the reflection of autumnal colors in their mirrored sunglasses. "It's kind of an annual sojourn, I guess. Coming up here, I mean."

"I get it." Evie gestured to the space around them. "It's gorgeous up here. Even just for the scenery. I totally get it."

There was a moment, as Maeve looked away, when Evie swore their face bore some confusion mixed with the bitter tang of loneliness. *Something* tugged at her then; a yank on her heartstrings.

Some truth of Maeve's recognized a truth in her.

"Want to share a boulder and a bit of bourbon?" they asked, motioning behind them. "I'm usually alone up here, but uh...don't feel like you have to run away."

"Yeah, I'd like that." Evie silently thanked her bleary-eyed common sense this morning for picking the sturdier boots out of her closet. She scrambled up the boulder and was almost to the top when a neatly manicured hand was thrust into her vision. "Thanks."

Maeve was strong. Really strong. They hauled her up like she weighed nothing and with one hand. If Evie had been the swooning type, she would have put a hand to her forehead and sighed. The thought made her chuckle. "Did I miss something?"

Evie shot them a toothy grin. "I just was thinking if someone this strong pulled me up a boulder and I were the swooning type, I might have defeated the purpose of your kind gesture."

Maeve stared at her for a long second then burst out laughing. "Shit, you're straightforward."

She grimaced. "Yeah, not one of my more redeeming qualities."

"No, it's good. A lot of people aren't like that." Maeve pushed their sunglasses up into that cloud of hair and Evie got a good look at dark brown eyes that were almost gold at the iris. "I like the forthrightness. Not a fan of dancing around people."

"I get it. Working the bar like that is a lesson in how to handle idiosyncrasies and assholes. Sometimes at the same time."

Something flashed again over Maeve's face before they handed her a heavy silver flask. The surface was mirror-polished and smooth to the touch. "Speaking from experience?"

Evie blew out a raspberry, took a sip. Took another sip. "Take your pick. I did the whole retail stint in high school, then through college. Clothing store in the mall, awful. Bookstore, marginally less awful but the managers sucked. Bar where the tips were good but the owner was too busy getting drunk to notice when the Friday night frat boys got too loud." She rolled her eyes. "So many calls to the cops because two meatheads decided to take their beef to the bathroom or alley." She handed the flask back with a nod. "And that's just brushing the surface."

"Hmmm, yeah, I get that." Maeve's thoughtful hum was a nice sound. They drank from the flask, their eyes locked on the horizon. The silence stretched, twisting only as a slight wind kicked up dead leaves and ruffled their hair. "I come up here because it was my wife's favorite spot in the entire world. We traveled a lot and we'd seen water so blue it hurt your eyes and mountain sunrises and little cobblestone plazas dotted with spring flowers. But she loved it here."

And then Maeve turned and pinned Evie in place with those eyes. "It was home. And no matter where we went, we always came back home. So now I come back here, every year, the day after she died."

The air left Evie's lungs. The grief of losing the one you held closest was a monster; a ravaging, raging, gluttonous beast that loved every tear, every memory, every dried funeral flower. She could say she was sorry - because she was - but that was to make *her* feel better. So few people knew what to do when someone else was mourning, but very rarely did they learn anything from their own brushes with death and loss. So she said what she wished others had said to her after she lost Sinclair. "You keep her memory well, then."

Maeve inhaled sharply. "You know that, too?"

"The grief? Yeah."

Maeve passed the flask back and as Evie grabbed it, their hands brushed. No one pulled away but Maeve gave her a curious look. Just a questioning cock of their head, but curious all the same. "Thanks. Good bourbon. I can tell you own a bar."

Maeve chuckled at that and said, "You're welcome. Thanks for hearing me out."

Evie smiled.

* * *

Evie's phone pinged the next morning.

From: Maeve
You need a job, right?

From: Evie
Yep. New town, new gig, need some cash.

From: Maeve
How good are you behind the bar?

Evie chuckled. How good was she? More like how bad she was going to make everyone else look. She'd been mixing drinks since she was fifteen; a lesson in basic mixology that was well earned after trying to make Long Island Iced Teas from her dad's liquor cabinet and spending the following day in the bathroom.

From: Evie
Do I need to pass a test to get a bartender job with you?

From: Maeve
If you've tended before, you know the drill.

A little thrill shivered down her spine. Maeve wasn't the flirty type, but the chance to get to know them better wasn't something she was about to turn down. Plus, you know, it was a job. Moving to Elsie was supposed to be a fresh start, a chance for growth and renewal. Niall had a sweet new gig at the engineering firm in the town over and he had fronted her some cash for a little apartment on the water. She wanted to pay him back with interest. And not just for the apartment, but for everything. For every time he'd pulled her out of some spot of trouble; for every job she had gotten fired from. For her two stints in rehab after Sinclair died.

Thank the gods alcohol had never been her go-to crutch when things got rough. She could make a mean cocktail, make some good tips, maybe make a friend or two. And pay her brother back for everything.

From: Evie
Count me in. Tell me the when and where and I'll be there.

* * *

Maeve eyed the line of perfectly made drinks. "Okay, you know your drinks. And you're fast. Now the true test."

Evie sucked in a breath, wiped her hands on her apron. "I'm ready."

They liked Evie. She was bold as brass with a tendency to run at the mouth a little; a nice contrast to their own stoicness. Being the more silent type wasn't a bad thing; people really did talk a lot around them and it made everything a bit simpler. Took some of the guesswork out of daily life. Stella had been their filter for a lot of that. She'd been so aware, so socially and emotionally intuitive; to Maeve it had seemed like witchcraft. It had been intimidating at first - hell, for a long time - but eventually they got into a rhythm. That rhythm became understanding, and by then they were so madly in love that anything was possible.

One of Stella's most important lessons - led by example, of course - was watching body language. So when they saw Evie suck in a quick breath and square her shoulders, Maeve knew she was ready. The old Maeve wouldn't have noticed such finer details. "Pick me or Carter to make a custom drink for."

Carter was at least eight inches taller than Evie, but he was doing his best to not look intimidating while he sat beside

Maeve at the bar. He was actually a giant teddy bear, prone to rib-crushing hugs when given permission and singing off key while wiping down bottles. But Maeve had needed their most experienced barkeep to run Evie through this little test. He had a great eye for talent and a more discerning one for potential issues.

"Ooh-kay…" Evie gave them a grin, but her shoulders were tense with nerves. "No offense, Carter, but I've known Maeve for about ten seconds longer than you. Familiarity wins out, even if you could bench press me."

Carter snorted before clapping Maeve on the shoulder. "I like her. Try not to scare her off, yeah? We need more help around here."

Evie's gaze turned expectant, but Maeve waved Carter off. "Yeah, yeah. Get out of here."

"Already halfway gone, boss."

Once Carter disappeared out the side door, Maeve said, "Whenever you're ready. No rush."

Evie sucked in another deep breath, but now Maeve watched her posture relax. "So, you're my new customer at the bar, that how we're playing this?"

"If you want."

That got a toothy smile and a spark in those curiously dark hazel eyes behind Evie's thick framed glasses. "Hell yes. I like roleplaying."

Maeve raised an eyebrow, but they had a hard time stopping the smile that crept over their face. "I'm afraid to ask."

"Okay fine, we'll call it *acting*."

"I thought that's what roleplaying was."

"Depends on the context." Evie was trouble. Maeve didn't usually like trouble. Maybe an exception could be made. "All right then. I guess I'll start." At Maeve's nod, Evie leaned forward, palms flat on the bar, and gave them a curious but non-invasive glance. "What's your favorite drink?"

They squinted at her. "Pretty sure that is cheating."

"No, I swear this has a point." She gestured to the polished cherry bar, the gleaming taps, the pristine bottles behind her. "And besides, if I fuck this up, then you'll know you don't want to hire me and you're out a bit of time but no real risk taken, right?"

Something inside Maeve twisted at the lost wistfulness in Evie's voice. It registered more forcefully than they expected. "All right. For the record, it's a Manhattan."

"Yes! Classic! I somehow knew it would be something so-phisticated but very easy to fuck up. So let's say you've already had the perfect Manhattan, but one more drink sounds like it would hit the spot. But you don't want something with the same flavor profile. You want something different. Unique." They got another look but this time, Maeve couldn't read the expression on Evie's face. Instead, they stared at the bumpy slope of her nose as she turned to the side and pulled out a rocks glass. "And I can fit it in this glass."

"Are you telling me or asking me?"

"A little of both." Evie plucked up the glass with a grin so wide it threatened to crack her face. "Got any fresh figs?"

They watched, astounded, as Evie made what she called a "Fig Street", her take on an old fashioned but with maple sugar and fresh fig juice and pulp. It was decadent but not rich; velvety smooth and not too heavy on the bourbon.

It was perfect.

Maeve lingered over a few sips of the drink Evie proudly placed before them, studying the deep amber liquid. "This is really good. I don't even like old fashioneds."

Evie gasped. "Blasphemy! You own a speakeasy! What do you mean you don't like old fashioneds?"

They had to chuckle at the faux outrage in her voice. Evie was probably a terrible poker player, given how quickly her face gave her emotions away. "If I'm drinking bourbon, I want it straight. Same for whiskey and good Scotch."

"You like your dark liquors, and you like the correct ones," Evie said slowly, quietly. "I do admire when someone knows their tastes that well."

"I was that weird college kid who preferred a nice, throaty single malt over whatever rainbow-colored nonsense everyone else was drinking." Maeve took another sip of the old fashioned, marveling at how the maple sugar transformed with the fig juice lent a slight sweetness without making the drink syrupy. "I guess I'm still weird."

"Nah. I know weird. My brother is weird. Brilliant, but weird. Our parents are dumb and weird and spend money like it's going out of style." Evie frowned and Maeve was given a glimpse of real hurt under her cavalier tone. "You're not weird. You're *refined*." She leaned forward more, elbows on the bar as she stared at Maeve. It wasn't intrusive; it was inquisitive. Honest. "You're fun. I like you."

Coming from anyone else, it would be an insult. Maeve wasn't the one you went to for a good time. That joke got old before the ink on the deed to the bar was dry.

Isn't it hilarious the old stick in the mud owns a bar? You ever seen them get wild, even once?

Maeve wouldn't know fun if it bit them on the ass.

Stella had thought they were fun, too. In their own, weird, *refined* way.

"Thank you." Maeve cleared their throat, looking for something to do other than down a strong cocktail. They fumbled with the chain around their neck, their fingers closing around the ring that hung there. Damn, that was a way too polite thing to say.

They wished Stella were here to help.

"Join me?"

They watched Evie blink twice then grin. That big, bright grin of hers that took up the lower half of her face and made laugh lines deepen pleasantly. "Okay, but I'm not drinking that. Not a bourbon fan."

"What's your weapon of choice?"

Evie plonked a bottle on the bar. "Ah Jose, my old friend."

Tequila was the devil. "Nope."

"Yes."

* * *

Maeve learned that night that Evie could chatter enough for both of them and she was an expert at drinking tequila slowly but steadily. Neither was drunk by one a.m., but it was a nice night for a walk down the beach. Just enough to let the pot of coffee and greasy eggs they'd downed at the diner sink in.

The waves were a soft lull against the chirping of crickets and the shine of a full moon. Picturesque, perfect. They had dozens of memories from over the years with Stella; on nights just like this and being roused from sleep to go walk the beach. The way Stella looked in that glittering, velvety light. The pull of her eyes and hands until Maeve was in her arms, safe and secure.

This could have been any of those nights. But it wasn't. Stella was gone but for once, they weren't alone.

Nice wasn't always a safe, boring thing. This was nice, the two of them sharing the beach and the moon and the sound of the waves.

But Evie wasn't looking at the water. She was staring down at the Lamplighter apron gripped in her hand. "I won't let you down, I swear."

"I don't think you will."

"Well, tell that to my parents? Niall is the only one who believes in me." Evie's knuckles went pale around the apron. "I have to pay him back. He's done so much for me." There was real heartbreak, real pain behind those words. A bit of her tone even cracked here and there and Maeve wanted to comfort her. But how did you do that with someone you barely knew?

But then Evie laughed and said, "Shit, here I am dumping on you when this all started with me interrupting your sojourn for Stella." She turned to Maeve with a fierce, sad expression. "Thank you for the job and the chance. You're a kind person."

They floundered for a long moment, torn between a simple nod and the words that fought to surface. "I uh...I'm shit at this. The emotions thing. Stella was always my guidepost for that." Maeve snorted, fighting with the contempt for their own lack of skill with words and feelings. "But I'm learning. I hope that's okay. And I'm glad you're here, Evie."

Now the woman turned to look at them and Maeve could see the dampness at the corner of her eyes. "Can I hug you?"

"Yeah."

Evie wrapped Maeve in a tight hug that smelled of honey

and cinnamon, her hair brushing their cheek. They brought their arms up and the moment that happened, Evie slumped forward with a sigh. "Thank you. I needed that."

"Yeah, me too."

To You, My Home, I Return

"Okay, okay um....so there was this guy who comes in the store today and he's all moping around cause he so doesn't want to be there." Yuri paused, remembering the man's sour face and how his hands were stuffed into his pockets. "And it's a perfume oil shop and this guy doesn't smell anything. Who does that?"

Beckett laughed. "Apparently someone who knows no joy in life."

"Yeah, yeesh. So Harriet's with someone else and Nu's behind the register busy, leaving me with this guy. I go over to see if he needs help and this dude says, 'About goddamn time, I've been here forever and no one has helped me.'" Yuri rolls his eyes even though Beckett can't see him. "What the hell?"

"Sounds like an asshole."

"Exactly! He was in the store two minutes tops. Harriet

doesn't like us immediately swarming people, which makes sense. But damn, dude."

"I'm sorry, babe. I know you were having a really good week."

Yuri hugged a pillow to his chest with his free hand, liking how the velvet felt against his skin. He tried not to think about how hard he was gripping the phone, as if he could physically hold Beckett close. "I'm not going to let some joyless jerk ruin it. I did have a good week. Thank you for the reminder."

Beckett hummed happily. "Of course. So what else happened?"

Yuri told her about exam prep and the new tea flavor Nu had made and how beautiful Elsie was now that the fall colors had come out in full. With Beckett across the country for school and Yuri at home, they made do with phone and video calls and texting rituals that kept Yuri from feeling too needy. He *missed* Beckett and they way she smelled like honey and how red-orange her hair was and how she liked oversized sweatshirts and never, ever wearing socks while inside. She'd be home soon for winter break but until then, he wrapped himself in the sounds of her laugh and the clink of a spoon against bone china. Jasmine green tea, every night.

"So how's the paper coming along?" he asked as he tangled

his fingers in the pillow's tassel. He used to get made fun of for liking "girly" things: smooth fabrics, knitting, any book or movie that didn't involve guns or mindless killing. But Beckett knew him and knew what he liked and so every time she came home to Elsie, she brought him a new tasseled pillowcase or a bright skein of yarn or a gay romance book they both had to read *now*.

Soon she would be home and staying with her moms and sneaking him onto the hill behind the mayor's office so they could sled ride like they were little kids and neighbors again.

Beckett was actually the love of his life. He knew people his age fell in and out love or lust easily and he got it. But for Yuri, Beckett was it. She was kind and funny and absolutely took no prisoners when someone pissed her off. She went to Pride parades before she could talk and her moms taught her to swear and drink in moderation and fostered a love of books and art and architecture. Beckett was so goddamn smart and he was fiercely proud of her going after her master's in engineering.

He listened as Beckett talked about the new research assignment she was hoping for and how the talk of campus was the hot new ethics professor. "I can't honestly tell you if they are or not!" Beckett said, laughing as he asked *how hot*. "Is this your subtle way of reminding me I should go outside on occasion?"

"No but now that you mention it....go outside *and* try to find Professor Gorgeous. You've got me curious."

Beckett snorted. "Well, apparently she's both very tall and and pretty ripped. I'd like to see her bench press some of those frat morons who would rather stand around all day talking about the weights they're going to lift."

"Hot."

"I know. Ah, shit, babe, I should probably go. I told Rita I'd help her with some library stuff and she wakes up too fucking early."

He'd braided all the tassels on the pillow while they'd been talking. He'd always been twitchy but it was worse when he was like this: a little sad, missing Beckett like crazy, but always so glad to hear her voice. "Yeah, okay."

"Four weeks."

"Four weeks," he repeated. "Oh and bug Audra again about what I should bring! They keep telling me they'll get back to me but...."

"You know how Mom is." Beckett paused. "I'm kind of hoping this is the year Sav gets them to consider retiring. They've worked their ass off for Elsie for years, they deserve their own time."

"And a vacation."

"One thing at a time,' Beckett said fondly. "Mom is not going to retire and then immediately turn into Karen Carnival Cruise."

The comment caught him just as he took a sip of water and he spluttered through a few seconds of damp laughter. "*Karen Carnival Cruise?!*"

"I said what I said!" But she was laughing, too.

They said goodbye and Yuri fell asleep with the phone in his hand like he always did after they talked.

* * *

Two weeks later

"Hey. I'm Jackson."

Nu's face was completely void of anything other than sterile politeness as he replied, "I'm Nu, that's Yuri. Nice to meet you, Jackson."

Without invitation, Jackson sat on the open barstool next to Yuri, wedging him in the middle. He cut his eyes to Nu, who was sipping his beer and still wearing that polite smile. Without a word, they had a quick conversation.

Did he just sit down?

He most definitely did, and right by you. It's not me he's after.

Fuck.

It must be so tough being handsome and smart and taken. Want me to tell him off?

Nah, maybe he's just being friendly.

He is definitely NOT only being friendly.

"So, uh, Yuri....you a townie or just in for the holidays?" Jackson was keeping his space *his* and not leaning into Yuri's, but by the scent of the man's cologne and the open neck of his button-down shirt, he figured it was only a matter of time. Better to nip this in the bud now.

"Elsie proud," Yuri replied lightly, clinking his glass with Nu's. "You?"

"Family's got a farm up on Bear Hook. I come back as much as I can, though."

"That must be nice."

"It is. My family's been trying to get me to move back but you get used to the city." Jackson laughed and Yuri had to admit it was a nice one, not too rough or warbly. Masculine, full-throated. "Dating in the city sucks ass, though."

"I can only imagine," Nu intoned. "I met my boyfriend here. Yuri met his girl here."

Yuri watched the man's face crumple and he felt bad, but other than sit beside him, Jackson hadn't actually done anything. What if he'd misread the entire situation? "So Bear Hook? You must have hiked that a billion times already."

To his credit, Jackson recovered quickly and was soon telling them about the time he and his brother tried to ski down Bear Hook hill, only to get caught by their grandmother. "God, that woman could shame you without yelling or even raising her voice even a little! We got in so much trouble for that stunt."

Nu laughed. "Sounds like my Auntie. If looks could skin you alive...."

"Harriet fucking adores you," Yuri shot back.

"You too, brat-lite."

Eventually Jackson moved on to more prospective pastures, leaving them to a final round of drinks. But Yuri still felt bad. It had taken a long time to fight against the impulse to curb his more "emotional" side; his stepmom never liked that he was a little too effeminate, a little too soft-spoken. She was long gone but she'd left his dad in a heap of PTSD, grief, and remorse and Yuri had to parent his grown father instead of dealing with his own shit. He was just now getting to it. "Hey, Jackson!"

The taller man turned with a small smile, Yuri's gaze going right to the open-neck shirt he'd mentally mocked not a half an hour ago. "Yeah?"

"It was nice talking to you. I'm sorry if you thought -"

Jackson held up a hand. "No worries. To be fair, I kind of figured a good looking guy like you would be taken but gotta try, right?"

A flash of insight - a gut feeling - rippled through him. Jackson was tall and graceful with a narrow face and dark brown, wavy hair swept off his high forehead. He was *exactly* what a friend of his was looking for. "Yeah, I get it. Really. I'm flattered."

Jackson's mouth twitched into a smile. "Sounds like you and your girl have been together for a while."

"Friends since second grade but then we did the whole classic *date everyone else but the one you should be with* scenario." Yuri grinned. "But in like the most bisexual way possible. She thought she was gay, I thought I was gay, but we both realized we actually love each other. Many a moment worthy of a teen dramedy was had."

"Tale as old as time!" Jackson replied, now giving him a full-wattage smile. "But I get it. And thanks."

"Sure, but that's not the only reason I came over. You seem nice, and I've got a friend, best bartender in Elsie." Yuri gave him The Lamplighter's name and address, then added, "And I'll let Carter know. I'm not about to surprise the guy."

"Yeah, totally. And thanks."

When he got back to his seat, Nu was turned sideways on the barstool and pressing a final beer into his hand. "Yes, and?"

"I mentioned Carter."

"And?"

"Guess we should ask Carter in a few days. Let me text him first, though."

Nu chuckled into his drink. "I swear, you hook more people up than anyone I've ever known. And you're good at it!"

"My true calling in life?"

"You wish."

Later that night, he and Beckett chatted over tea in their pajamas. "How's Nu?"

"Nu is over the damn moon with Miles."

"Those two, I swear. From the moment you told me about Nu fawning over the hottie at the coffee shop, I knew they were both done for."

"Honestly, I've never seen him so happy."

"Oh no, are they one of *those* couples already?"

Yuri laughed. "I don't know how they aren't. They're fucking adorable."

Beckett made a few fake gagging noises over the line but then laughed. She loved Nu like a brother and Yuri knew the moment she and Miles met, the two of them would be talking about arcade games and poetry. "Anything else wild happen? Or even remotely interesting?"

"I got hit on at the bar. I think."

"Yuri."

"Huh?"

"You *think*? Babe, I know we've both been out of the dating game for a while but I'm pretty sure you can tell when someone's trying to flirt with you."

He undid one of the braided tassels on the pillow, letting the soft strands fall between his fingers. "It was all very subtle. Sat beside me, addressed me first, but was nice to Nu. I don't know."

Beckett was quiet for a moment. "You okay?"

"Yeah. Anyways, he backed off the minute he got told I had someone and honestly, I think he and Carter might hit it off."

"Oooo, matchmaking at the bar. You are weirdly good at that. And hey, you sure you're okay?"

He sighed and flopped back on the bed. They'd video called that morning before Beckett's TA session and his shift at Twelfth Moon, but tonight the ache of loneliness was a weight in his chest. "Just miss you. I know we've only got a couple weeks before you're home but it feels like time is intentionally dragging."

"I miss you too. I always do. Thank god for cell phones and the internet." She laughed and it made something near his heart soar. "But just wait, the Moms are already planning about ten massive meals. Very intent on feeding you until you pass out from a food coma."

Yuri could already taste Audra's roast chicken and broccoli salad and Savanna's apple pie. Beckett's moms were really good people and Yuri had known them for so long, he saw them as family. They'd taken him in after his own mother passed away from cancer and his dad ran off with his mistress, only to come back with a stepmom for Yuri.

But Audra and Savanna...They treated him like a friend and a son and their daughter's boyfriend all in one swoop. He'd get random texts from Savanna asking about his cat, Tricksy, and photos from Audra of the newest recipe they'd tried out. And they had him come over for dinner or brunch, whether Beckett was home or not. It lessened the loneliness some, but of late everyone was so busy he'd felt a tad on the outside.

It was no one's fault. He was shit about reaching out and even worse about actually following through on dinner party plans or nights out at the bar he concocted in his head. Maybe he should get out more, meet new people. The comic shop had a weekly board game night...

He heard the sound of a spoon on a saucer and smiled. Beckett was a creature of habit during stressful times and her nightly tea routine was oddly soothing to his ears. He could picture her seated cross-legged in her chair, phone on the little desk in her apartment's bedroom while she sipped jasmine oolong. Her red hair would be in a long braid hiked over one shoulder, or loose and wavy from being pulled up all day, and she'd have on some ratty sweatshirt and shorts, her feet bare.

Fuck, he missed her. The desire to pull her close, hold her, kiss that spot under her ear that made her go limp.

"Yuri?"

He jolted up, the phone nearly slipping from his grasp. "Yeah, yeah! I'm here! Sorry, drifted off."

"You need to get some rest, sir." Beckett's voice was soft, lulling. "I love you. Go to bed."

"I love you, too."

He was out soon afterwards but awoke in the middle of the night, unable to go back to sleep. Instead he slipped out of bed, flinching against the cold floor, and stood before the window. Snow had begun to fall in a powdery curtain and Tricksy was content to watch it from the window seat. "Just a handful more days," he said softly, scratching the cat behind the ears. "And then she'll be here until spring."

Tricksy purred at him before licking the side of his hand. "Ooof, bedhead," he groaned as he tousled his hair and made a mental note to get a haircut before Beckett came home.

* * *

"Just come in!"

Yuri chuckled. Savanna always said that but he'd always felt weird simply walking into her and Audra's home. "I brought wine, that grants me entry, right?"

Savanna appeared in the doorway and grinned at him. "Honey, anyone bringing wine to our house is welcome. But especially you." She pulled him into a tight hug, smelling of butter and vanilla and he slumped. "Ah, rough week?"

"Busy," he muttered into her shoulder. The blue sweater she wore was soft under his cheek. "Store's so full of holiday shoppers cause everyone waits until the last minute."

Savanna laughed. "You and Beckett might be the only people I know outside of Harriet who don't procrastinate on that stuff."

Yuri pulled his head up to stare down at her, taking in her little half-moon glasses and the scar along her jaw she got while in the military. "Oh, speaking of Harriet...." He dug into his bag and pulled out a neatly wrapped package. "She sent along some samples, said you'd both enjoy them."

Savanna's grin grew wider. "I love that woman."

And then Audra's face appeared over Savanna's shoulder. They had a smudge of flour on their cheek and a bit of it in the pile of dark red hair pulled into a bun on top of their head. "Are you making him freeze?"

"No, we're chatting."

Audra kissed her temple. "While freezing. Don't let her do that, Yuri."

Yuri let himself be led into their cozy home that smelled of warm apple pie and immediately he relaxed. This was home, too, and he loved it here; full of books and instruments and art. Savanna was a ceramicist and she had her own home studio and a thriving business across the coastline and far west. Audra's role as town mayor certainly helped Savanna's business, but her career had long been established before they were ever married.

Yuri soon had a glass of mulled cider in one hand, a cookie in the other, and was on the couch cooing at the Westmark dog, Scottie. Named after the Star Trek character, not the terrier breed. Scottie was some indeterminate mutt who acted like a Husky but looked like a cross between that and a retriever. "What can I do?"

"Not a thing!" Savanna said over her shoulder as she and Audra moved around the open plan kitchen with ease. The ease of two people used to each other, used to working with and around each other. Like he wanted to be with Beckett one day.

Yuri shook his head just as Scottie plopped his big muzzle into his lap. "Whoa, watch buddy! I don't want to spill this on you. Here." He sat the mug aside while Scottie snuffled at his pants for cookie crumbs. "I don't think that's good for you."

"It's not but he does it anyways." Beckett was leaning against the far wall, grey eyes bright in her angular face. "And I told you I missed you."

Yuri was launching himself at her not a second later, barely mindful of the fact that Beckett's parents were watching him scoop her up into a hug brimming with shocked, delighted laughter. "Holy shit. Holy shit."

"Surprise."

He wanted to melt into the floor from sheer happiness. "How - why - "

"I missed you. I love you. I made it work." She ran her thumbs over his cheeks in that oh so familiar way; it made his heart wrench to fully comprehend how much he had missed her. That simple touch was threatening to buckle him at the knees.

He turned with her in his arms to see Savanna and Audra grinning widely. "You two."

"No idea what you're talking about," Audra said before turning back to the simmering pots on the massive stove.

"No idea at all." Savanna winked before joining her spouse, her face alight with joy as she resumed her stirring.

"I can't believe you're here," he breathed out, his heart hammering hard in his chest. "You....sneak!"

"You love it," she countered. "Mom got me on an early flight. Apparently they know a few pilots? News to me."

Yuri rested his forehead against hers. "You're here."

Her hug threatened his air supply but he welcomed it. "I am."

Thank you for purchasing this book!

For more information on Halli's books, visit hallistarling.com. There is a volume two planned for Elsie and its residents! Be on the lookout for that in 2022.